A Home for Mandy

by
Janet Baughman

Janet Baughman

Huntington House Publishers

Huntington House Publishers
P.O. Box 53788
Lafayette, Louisiana 70505

PRINTED IN THE UNITED STATES OF AMERICA.

Library of Congress Card Catalog Number 2002115584
ISBN 1-56384-199-1

Dedication

To women everywhere, both young and old, who find themselves in adverse circumstances. Remember, you are special. Do not give up or settle for second best. God has a wonderful plan for your life.

Acknowledgments

Portions of the material describing the Rev. John Adger's life were taken from his autobiography *My Life and Times*. Some of the vignettes and descriptions of houses and characters in the Charleston section of this book were taken from the booklet "60 Famous Houses of Charleston, S.C.," published by the News and Courier of Charleston, S.C. First and foremost this book is a work of fiction, therefore whereas some names may be recognizable, character development has been strictly a figment of my imagination.

Janet Baughman

Chapter One

❋ _____

Tennessee, 1850

One by one a thousand needles seemed to pierce her legs as the ants fiercely protested her presence. Mandy bit her lips to keep from screaming.

"I'm safe here, I'm safe here," she chanted to herself as she shrank deeper into the cavern that she had dug under the chicken coop. Chicken droppings, spiders, and beetles shared her space, but the red ants were the worst. Still, Jeb would never think of looking for her here. The blackberry canes she had piled up at the opening served to discourage both man and beast.

Ever since the death of her mother, the drunken rages of her stepfather had escalated until they had become unbearable. Survival was the name of the game, now. She could hear his harsh breathing and raspy cough as he shouted her name from the dilapidated porch of their frame house with its rotting, unpainted boards and broken windows.

"Call all you want, Jeb," she muttered. "You're never going to see me again." Mandy had been planning her escape for days; squirreling away scraps of food and small coins in a faded pillowcase made from a flour sack. Even her one good dress, a blue cotton with white crocheted lace collar and cuffs, had been carefully folded into the sack along with a pair of homemade sandals. The only remembrance from her mother, a small silver cross, hung around her neck on a piece of ribbon. Mandy had a habit of fingering it when she was nervous.

"Whenever trouble finds you, call on God," her ma had often said, but Mandy wasn't so sure. Where had He been when her ma died after she had fallen trying to escape her husband's drunken wrath, and where was God now when she needed Him? She shifted her legs noiselessly to rub the itching bites. Why did good people like her ma suffer the torments of people like Jeb?

"God made man in His image; that makes man special. Woman came later to serve and obey man," Jeb constantly reminded Mandy and her ma as he worked them day and night in the fields. Mandy had watched her ma's face take on a haggard look with sunken eyes, sallow complexion, and dry, brittle hair. Ma had become like a puppet, shuffling here and there under her husband's commands, receiving a hearty slap if she was not fast enough. Mandy scowled at the memory. Perhaps death had been a relief to her ma, a means of escape.

"Death is not for me, no siree! I'll show that old coot! I'm going to be free and do what I want. No more hoeing in the hot sun til I drop, or hauling water, or cleaning the chicken coop. I'm going to be a lady with fine clothes and a fancy house. No man's gonna boss me around ever! Mandy's a queen bee!" Mandy clenched her fists to emphasize her resolution, then carefully peeked between the berry canes to monitor the situation.

The alcohol's numbing effects had gotten the best of Jeb who was slumped in the torn striped canvas of an old lawn chair. After what seemed an eternity, Mandy crept from her dusty lair and, clutching the sack containing her worldly goods, silently crept along the fence line. She weaved in and out of weeds and brush in an attempt to remain invisible. A cool breath of air welcomed her as she entered the woods that bordered their property. Safe at last! She often roamed through this green canopy of pines with its spicy aroma and soft pine needle floor. Several miles later a small spring-fed pond bordered by mossy rocks waited just around a curve in the path. This was her thinking spot. She came here as often as possible to dream and scheme. The dappling effect of the sun shining through the trees made the water look as though it were covered with golden coins.

Mandy set her sack down and took off her blouse and skirt. The pond bottom was muddy, and she hated the feel of the ooze between her toes, so she kept on her tattered leather boots. With a little shiver she waded into the cool water. Making a small scrubber from a handful of reeds, she washed herself thoroughly from top to bottom.

"I'm washing away the past. I don't want one speck of my old life left," she said, squeezing droplets from her long, brown hair. Emerging from the water, she whirled around and around with outstretched arms until she was damp dry and breathless. Then she took her ragged clothes and scrubbed them until there was hardly a thread left. She draped them over a bush in a sunny spot, and they dried quickly in the afternoon heat.

As the evening stillness crept over the forest, Mandy turned aside from the path she had been following and withdrew a bacon biscuit from her bag, an old towel to lie on, and her hair brush. The biscuit crumbled with age, but since she could eat it in peace, it tasted delicious. Next she brushed and braided her hair, then with a sigh of contentment, surrendered to the lullaby of the night creatures.

In the predawn haze, Mandy woke with a start. She

could hear the rustle of leaves as footsteps came down the path! Grabbing her towel and sack, she crept under an alder bush, waiting with bated breath as the footsteps came closer. She almost laughed out loud in relief as she saw a doe and her fawn appear from the underbrush. Now wide awake, she realized she was cold. There was no use trying to go back to sleep when walking would warm her, so she rolled up her towel, stuffed it in her sack, and began to trek south.

"Pendleton, South Carolina, here I come, ready or not," she sang out to the sleeping birds. "Pendleton, O Pendleton, please be good to me. Pendleton, O Pendleton, a cousin I'm going to see." Mandy giggled at her attempt at rhyming and walked faster. She had once heard her ma talk about the prestigious Drake family of Charleston and mention that a cousin, Cornelia Greene Drake, had a summerhouse in Pendleton. Mandy was related to the Greenes on her mother's side, but she wasn't sure of the exact family connection.

All she knew was that many of the people from the Low Country of South Carolina came to the mountains in the summer to avoid the "summer sickness." No one knew what caused the symptoms, but people often died a horrible death from the disease or else spent the rest of their life having ague attacks. She had to reach Pendleton while it was still summer, but she had no idea how long it would take her to walk there. Well, it didn't matter; anything was better than living in Tennessee on that poor excuse for a farm and a crazy man for a stepfather.

Chapter Two

The sun was boring a hole into her head. Water, she needed water. Her tongue felt swollen and fuzzy; her breath came in short pants. Spots danced before her eyes. Mandy had been walking for five days. She had long since eaten her scraps of food. Precious time was spent looking for late season, wild strawberries and dewberries to quiet her demanding stomach. She was so thirsty. Why hadn't she thought to bring a container for water? She had resorted to soaking her towel in a stream and wringing a few drops from it at a time to slake her thirst, but the heat caused the towel to dry quickly. She felt desperate for a drink, and she was so tired! The rocky road she had been traveling wreaked havoc with her already worn out boots. Now she had holes in the soles as well as on top of the toes. Her bruised feet protested every step.

Mandy had followed the southern fork in the road for a day and a half without seeing a soul. Walking was lonely without a companion or even a dog to talk to. She once had a small, terrier type dog named Wags, but after her ma died Jeb shot it, because he said he couldn't afford to feed an extra mouth. Mandy knew he was lying. He just wanted to make life more miserable for her. Oh well, that was all over now. Impulsively, she stopped and wrote in the dust of the road the numbers from one to thirteen.

Then she deliberately stomped on them, wiping them out with the edge of her shoe. There! The first thirteen years of her life were completely obliterated. Closing her eyes, she imagined herself dressed in a shimmering white gown. In her hand was a magic wand to turn every good dream into reality. She would be beautiful; she would be rich; she would have a fancy house and servants that said, "Yes, ma'am."

"What do rich people do?" she wondered out loud. "I know, I'll have a house full of children, and we'll have sugar cake every night." Suddenly she stumbled over a rock and was jolted back to reality. The sun was making her daft, she thought. Rounding a bend in the road she saw an oak tree with large spreading branches offering welcome shade. She sat under its comforting coolness and soon drifted into a restless sleep.

"Mercy! What a ragamuffin!" proclaimed a shrill voice that penetrated Mandy's nap. "Child, are you sick or hurt? Wake up! Show some respect for your elders!"

"Water," Mandy croaked as she slowly opened her eyes.

"Big Jim, get her into the buggy," ordered the lady with the shrill voice to a muscular black man driving the horses. Big Jim gently picked up Mandy and her sack, and deposited her on the floor of the buggy. Then, cracking a whip, he urged the matched bays into a swift trot, which made their elegant heads bob in unison. After a few minutes, a small driveway veered to the right amid a stand of oaks and pines. From a distance, the two-story house with the large columns supporting a roofed verandah looked imposing, but when the buggy stopped near the front entry, Mandy saw the once elegant dwelling was in dire need of paint and repairs.

"I'll git you water, missy," said Big Jim, jumping from the buggy and hurrying to a covered well. Soon she was gulping the cool, sweet liquid, letting it trickle down her chin. The last bit in the cup she used to douse the dust and sweat off her face. Somewhat revived, Mandy climbed from the buggy and stood uncertainly by the sagging gate of a termite-eaten picket fence.

"You're too filthy to come into the house," shrilled the lady, "but if you go to the back door, I'll see you get fed."

Mandy slowly walked around the side of the house, passing a scraggly grape arbor and a small, weedy garden. To one side of the garden several peach trees covered with blight offered small, unripe fruit. Everything seemed shabby and neglected in contrast to the buggy and horses that shone with polished care.

"It wasn't always like this," said the lady, noticing Mandy's glances. "When Daddy was living the farm was neat and prosperous. Mama's shelves overflowed with canned goods. We had meat every day. She was famous around here for her biscuits and sausage gravy. But then the solicitor came saying the taxes hadn't been paid. Daddy and he got into an argument, and the next thing you know they were dueling in the early morning mist. Daddy died a week later from an infection caused by the bullet wound. Mama died of overwork and grief a few years later. Now it's just me and Big Jim and the matched bays that were Daddy's pride and joy. Sooner or later death will claim us all; in the meantime we do the best we can with what was left after we sold all the valuables to pay those cussed taxes." With that explanation she placed a plate of cold cornbread and greens into Mandy's outstretched hands. Mandy ate slowly and carefully to show the lady that she also had manners and breeding. When the last crumb was consumed, she handed the plate back with a prim "Thank you, Ma'am."

"Call me Miss Ellie," the woman commanded. "Now let's get the nits and bugs off of you. Take this soap over

to that rain barrel and scrub every inch of yourself, including your hair. Throw those rags you're wearing in a heap.
I'll find something else for you to put on. Land sakes,
you're so dirty and sunburnt I can't even tell what color
you are." After pointing Mandy in the direction of the
wash area, Miss Ellie turned with a swish of her faded
gingham skirt to search the treasures of an old chest for
some appropriate clothing.

Mandy did as she was told. The homemade lye soap
was strong and did not give much lather, but she applied
it with vigor. She left the soap in her hair until she had
completely finished washing her body, hoping it would
indeed rout the pests who had been holding court there.
The strong lye stung the bites and scratches she had ac-
cumulated in her travels, but it also served to flush out any
infection. Miss Ellie reappeared carrying a worn towel, a
soft cotton nightgown, and a cord belt. Since Mandy was
tall for her age, the nightgown, when belted, was just the
right length. She rummaged in her sack for her hairbrush.

"Don't use that; you'll just reinfest your head," warned
Miss Ellie when she saw the brush. "Here's a wide toothed
comb. Make do." Mandy slowly combed the tangles out
of her hair, wincing when she hit an especially matted
area. When it was all combed smoothly, she let it hang
straight to dry.

"You may come in now." Miss Ellie held the shuttered door open as Mandy entered the kitchen. Like many
southern houses built before the Civil War, the kitchen
was really a small separate room that adjoined the main
house by a trellised walkway. This feature protected the
principal dwelling from fire in case something in the
kitchen went awry. The scraped dirt floor covered with
river rocks offered cool relief to her blistered feet. Exhausted, she sat limply on a wooden bench.

"Poor thing, you're plumb tuckered out. You can sleep
in here tonight. I'll bring you a blanket. There'll be no

more cooking today, so you can rest undisturbed." Minutes later Miss Ellie dropped a corn husk mattress and ragged quilt at Mandy's feet. Both smelled musty, but Mandy was too tired to care. Mumbling her thanks, she surrendered to sleep.

Once she was sleeping deeply, the dream she had been having occasionally began to play itself out. She was standing by a wrought iron gate. Behind her was a spacious, brick, Georgian-style house set among large branching trees. She was wearing a blue gingham dress and white apron. The curious part came next. She seemed to be waving and calling to someone to come home. The dream was pleasant, so it did not disturb her and had recurred often enough that her mind was used to it. Sighing gently, she rolled over and continued sleeping.

The morning star was still shining in the rosy dawn sky when Mandy awoke to the sound of metal banging against metal.

"Coffee and grits is the breakfast fare," said Miss Ellie, tersely. "Course it's not real coffee; chicory and roots make it tasty, though." Grits were fine with Mandy as she had awoken with a hearty appetite. She stirred some dark honey into the creamy, white goo then got down to the business of eating.

"I don't mind feeding you, but you'll have to work for your board and keep. You're not from here, are you? The farms are scattered in these hills, but I think I know all the families that have girls your age." Miss Ellie looked appraisingly at Mandy. She was mighty thin, but there was a look of resourcefulness about her, and she seemed healthy enough. "She'll make a good field hand to help plant tobacco and greens and anything else I can sell," she decided.

Mandy pretended she had not heard a word the woman said. Her past was gone, and nobody was going to make

her discuss it again—ever! Finishing her grits, she carefully wiped her mouth with the worn napkin that had
been placed by her bowl. She was still hungry, but one
look revealed this house held no present abundance. All
the good times were past history. Miss Ellie pushed a
faded cotton blouse and well-worn skirt in her direction.

"This is about all I've got that will fit you. I couldn't
find any bloomers." Mandy nodded her thanks and looked
for a private place in which to change clothes.

"Go into the house, take the first door to the left, go
upstairs, and use the center room," instructed Miss Ellie.
"Be quick about it. We've got work to do. Big Jim is
plowing the small field, which I want to plant before it
rains."

Mandy slowly climbed the narrow, winding back stairs.
"I'll work two days to pay for her kindness, then it's on to
Pendleton," she said to herself. The upstairs rooms were
small and spare, but the center one had a window that
overlooked the front yard. A bed, dresser, and chamber
pot were the only furnishings. Above the dresser was an
oval mirror in a walnut frame. Mandy hurried to it. She
had not seen her image in a mirror since her mother had
remarried. Her stepfather, calling them instruments of
vanity, had broken every mirror in the house. She stared
at her reflection in the wavy glass. "I look like Ma," she
said with surprise, pulling her hair back. Her face was
long; her straight, brown hair came together in front in a
widow's peak; and high cheekbones accented large, dark
blue eyes. Her lips were thin but neatly shaped, framing
a wide smile that exposed small, even teeth.

"Oh, ma, help me! What am I to do? Why did you
die? I need you!" An achy lump rose in her throat, threatening to choke her. For a brief moment, tears filled her
eyes, but she shook her head fiercely to sweep them away.
"Ma's dead, girl! She can't help you. You're on your own.

Whatever you decide is what will be." A ray of sunlight slipping through the dirty window glinted on the silver cross around her neck. Mandy stroked it gently and felt comforted. She donned the blouse and skirt, wrapped the cord belt from her nightgown around her waist to hold everything together and went to report to Miss Ellie.

Chapter Three

The next two days taxed Mandy to the point of desperation. Setting the tobacco plants in the rich loam almost broke her back. Then, hauling water from the creek a quarter of a mile away to keep them alive almost pulled her arms from their sockets. The seedlings oozed a sticky, smelly substance that stained her fingers. Scrub as hard as she could, the smell and stain just wouldn't completely go away.

The third day Mandy made plans to leave. She searched the house for the sack containing her good dress but couldn't find it. Perhaps Miss Ellie had thrown it away. She hated to leave without her dress and towel, but go she must. She was wearing her sandals, and they seemed comfortable enough for serious walking. She took her nightgown and an old enamel berry pail she had found, considering them a fair trade for all the work she had done. Then, when Miss Ellie was occupied inside the house, she hurried down the road keeping to the shrubs along the side until the farm was out of sight. She was worse off now than when she had started her journey, not having even the towel to sleep on. She hoped Pendleton was not far away.

The next several days were spent walking and looking for food. Mandy found dewberries along the road and picked a pail full. One night she passed a farm that had a garden near the road. She helped herself to as many green beans as she could carry in the tail of her blouse. They were immature and not very tasty but filling. Now the wagon path turned into a gravel road. She saw a wooden sign propped against a rock. She guessed it was the name of a nearby town. Her ma had begun to teach her to read, but when her stepfather arrived all schooling stopped. She knew the alphabet but couldn't make sense of the word: S-Y-L-V-A.

After several hours, she came upon a group of log houses scattered in a small valley. Before she knew it, she was standing in front of a large building, which she guessed was a general store. People were entering with woven baskets or sacks in which to carry their purchases. She walked to a nearby alley where she could watch without being in the way. The sun was gathering strength, so she stepped up close to a building that offered shade. Whoosh! A bucket full of water and table scraps drenched her from head to toe.

"Hey!" Mandy yelled at the figure by the open window. "Watch what you're doing!" A woman's flushed face appeared at the opening. "Goodness gracious, girl. Don't you know better than to stand under an open kitchen window? Come 'round back and git cleaned up." Flicking potato peels and onionskins out of her hair, Mandy walked to the back of the building.

"You look worse than a cat in the middle of a dog fight. Where did you git those clothes, in your grannie's attic? Phew, that slop water sure didn't help your smell none!" Clucking like a mother hen, the lady—all two hundred pounds of her—poured fresh water into a metal basin and thrust it, some soap and a towel in Mandy's direction. "I run a boarding house and eatery," she continued. "I don't let anyone inside my establishment 'til they've washed up. That's why I keep these facilities on the back porch. You clean up as best you can. I'll see if I can find you some decent clothes. My name is Mrs. Dalrymple, but folks call me Mrs. D." With that brief introduction, she waddled into the house, the louvered door slamming behind her.

Mandy shut her eyes, took a deep breath, and plunged her whole face into the basin. The soap was good quality with a pleasing fragrance, so she lathered her hair, face, and neck. By the time she had washed and dried as much as she could without removing her clothes, Mrs. D had returned carrying a navy blue serge dress with a wide, white collar and mother of pearl buttons down the bodice.

"Believe it or not, I used to be just about your size years ago," she chuckled. "But my husband wanted a wife with some meat on her bones, so I obliged. Now he's dead, and I can't seem to stop eating. Step into the pantry and change your clothes. I was keeping this material to use for a chair cover, but you need it more than I do."

The dress fit nicely. Mandy was grateful for her height. If she had to wear castoffs, at least they didn't drag on the ground calling attention to her poverty-stricken state. She smoothed her hair as best she could and fixed it into one long braid.

"Well, you look almost human," remarked Mrs. D. "That dress sure brings out the blue of your eyes. Tell you what, you help me serve dinner today, and you can eat for free, not that you have any money, I'd guess. The gents around here would appreciate a fresh, young face."

Mandy nodded. She would do just about anything for a good meal. Following Mrs. D's example, she set the long table in the dining room with shiny silverware and cream colored napkins. My, it did look elegant! She wished she had some flowers to put on the table for a finishing touch. As the dinner hour approached and the hungry men appeared (with hands and faces spotless thanks to the wash area on the back porch), Mandy placed bowl after bowl of mashed potatoes, grits, ham, gravy, biscuits, cooked greens, beans, and stewed apples on the table. Dessert was dewberry-dried apple pie or molasses cake with raisins. She was almost faint with hunger, and everything smelled so appetizing. As soon as the meal was over and she had cleared the table, she heaped a plate with leftovers and sat down to enjoy the first decent meal she had had in months.

"Are you coming or going?" asked Mrs. D, easing her great weight onto the tressle bench, a cup of steaming hot coffee in her hand.

"Going," answered Mandy, shoveling a fork full of grits and gravy into her mouth.

"T'aint none of my business, but seems a pretty girl like you would be lookin' to settle somewhere, so's she could find a future husband. There are some mighty fine families here in Sylva. 'Course most of them are of Scottish decent, but you could do a lot worse."

Mandy shook her head . . . nosey woman. She'd never get a story from her to feed the town gossips. She averted her eyes and kept on eating. Realizing further questioning was fruitless, Mrs. D finished her coffee in silence and shuffled to the kitchen to begin washing dishes.

"You need to put some flesh on your bones before you start off again," she remarked. "If you will help me for a while, I'll outfit you for your journey, no questions asked." Mandy thought that sounded reasonable. There was no use traveling in a weakened condition and catching her death. She carried her plate to the sink and silently began to dry the silverware. When the kitchen was neatened, Mrs. D showed Mandy to a tiny, second story room under the eaves that contained a narrow bed and a clothes rack.

"Call this home for a while," she said, laying fresh linens on the bed. "If you work steady, I'll try to find you another dress, and some shimmies. A good pair of walking shoes won't hurt none, neither," she added, glancing at Mandy's dusty toes peeking through her sandals.

The next week went by in a blur. Rising at five A.M., Mandy helped cook and serve a hearty breakfast, then boiled laundry and hung it to dry. Next, it was time to prepare dinner. Mrs. D discovered Mandy could make a good pie crust, so she put her in charge of the desserts. The dusting and sweeping was done while the pies were baking. How Mrs. D managed to maintain her excess weight was a mystery to Mandy, who was eating like a horse but didn't seem to add a pound.

By the end of the first week, she had met all the regular boarders and could smile at their jokes. She learned which men wanted cream or sugar in their coffee and tried to anticipate their needs. Several gentlemen showed their appreciation by occasionally giving her a few pennies. She thanked them politely then put the coins in a cloth bag and hid it under a loose floorboard in her room. True to her word, Mrs. D rewarded her labors by giving her another secondhand dress: a dark, red wool that was too hot for summer wearing, and a petticoat with matching bloomers. Mandy felt downright prosperous.

"How far is it to Pendleton, South Carolina?" Mandy asked one day as she snapped beans at the kitchen sink.

"Not far. You can get there in a week or two, easy," replied Mrs. D, although she wasn't sure where the town was located. She guessed Pendleton was Mandy's destination, but she didn't want her to leave the boarding house any time soon. Life had gotten almost enjoyable with an extra hand to shoulder much of the load. "If you stay awhile longer, I'll see about getting you shoes."

Mandy needed sturdier shoes. The road was rocky, and small pebbles were constantly rolling into her sandals, irritating her feet. "I'll need stockings, too," she replied.

By the end of her third week in Sylva, she was feeling as though she belonged. Even girls her own age whose families came to dinner after church services now smiled at her with friendly eyes. Yet, she yearned for her own kin with whom she could share personal secrets. Her need for security would not be denied; she must find her cousin as soon as possible.

Finally, the day dawned when Mandy was free to resume her journey. Mrs. D had given her an old leather satchel left years before by some guest, and in it were resting her new dress, her sandals, and her money plus an old blanket and some personal items from the boarding house supplies. Breakfast that day was a regular party as the boarders crowded around to wish her a safe journey and press coins into her hand. Mrs. D filled a sack with ham slices, biscuits, loaf bread, fried apple pies, and dried fruit. For the first time, Mandy felt really prepared to travel. Sam, the blacksmith, had offered to take her the first five miles in his wagon since he had to repair a buggy axle at a farm in the general direction she was going. Waving good-by to her new friends, she was filled with optimism. The rest of the trip would be a breeze.

"Be careful walking about these parts," Sam warned as they rode along. "They be a lot of mountain men tucked away 'round here. They brew corn likker and act half crazy, especially when theys drinkin'. It's best to stay outta sight of man 'n beast. Here's the south road fork. Good luck, Miss Mandy. You know yer welcome in Sylva anytime."

"I'll be extra careful, Mr. Sam. Thank you for the ride," Mandy replied as she climbed from the wagon, clutching her precious satchel. According to Mrs. D, she hadn't that much farther to travel. How bad could it get?

Chapter Four

That afternoon the summer drought broke with a fury. Rain poured from dull, grey skies, and lightening bounced from ridge to ridge followed by deafening crashes of thunder. Mandy scurried under a hemlock tree with low hanging branches. Within minutes she and her belongings were soaked. After several hours of pelting rain, the storm moved on, leaving a blood-red sun, which promised a better day tomorrow.

"Red sun at night, sailor's delight," Mandy quoted as she picked her way around puddles and fallen tree limbs. She was too wet to rest comfortably, so she walked by the light of a full moon until she came to a meadow. Here some of the grass had been trampled down, probably by sleeping deer. She picked a soft clump and slept.

Every day seemed the same to her now: follow the road up a mountain, a climb that seemed determined to exhaust her, then down, down, down usually to a small valley with a rocky creek where fish played under small waterfalls. Occasionally, she would see a log cabin in the distance or pass a wagon on the road. At these times, she walked hidden among the trees. Her food was gone. Only her personal belongings, the coins, a blanket, and a small skinning knife that one of the men insisted she take "just in case" were left in the satchel. "Just in case of what?"

Mandy had questioned at the time. Now she knew. Just in case she caught an animal to eat, just in case she needed a branch for a walking stick, just in case of snake bite, just in case of danger.

Almost every afternoon, a summer storm rolled across the hills and valleys bringing with it lightening so bright and close you could thread a needle in its light. She was used to it now. Searching out a protective rock formation, cave or hemlock tree, she huddled with arms across her chest and head down until it was over. Then she walked until her clammy clothes dried from the heat of her body. Insects were a constant torment. Deer flies, black flies, and gnats pestered her during daylight hours while mosquitoes feasted on her flesh at night. Still she walked, urged on by her recurring dream and the desire for family.

One morning as she neared the crest of an especially steep, rocky section of the road, she heard a horse drawn wagon coming from the opposite direction. Quickly, she searched for a hiding place. Because of the rocks and height, there were few trees, and the shrubs were stunted. She crouched between an outcropping of boulders, pressing herself close to the ground. The horse appeared first, a scrawny beast snorting and blowing with the effort of the uphill climb. On the ancient wagon sat a thin man with bushy hair and matted beard. An old felt hat shaded his face from which streams of brown tobacco juice ejected periodically. The wagon was full of clay jugs, banging and rattling in protest of being bumped over the rocky trail. Because the rocks obstructed her view, Mandy remained hidden until she could no longer hear the wagon or its noisy contents. As she carefully stood up she found herself staring into a pair of watery grey eyes!

"Wal, lookie here! I got me a new wife," chortled a reedy voice as a brown, bony hand reached for her shoulder. With a shriek, Mandy flung herself backward away from his grasp. Suddenly, the earth rolled beneath her as the loose gravel started a rockslide, which carried her faster and faster down the sheer face of the mountain. At first she tried to stay upright, grabbing at protruding rocks or roots as she slid past, but soon speed became her enemy, and she tumbled sideways amid plummeting stones, until she landed with a thud on a small ledge. For a long time, she lay motionless. Every breath was agony. There was a dull ache in her right shoulder, and her body sang a song of pain and bruising. Finally, she moved her arms and wiggled her toes. Nothing seemed broken, so she attempted to sit up. Immediately, pain sliced through her like a knife, causing her to collapse. "I must have broken some ribs," she thought, taking small, shallow breaths. "I'll just have to lay here until they heal a bit." She eased her body into a more comfortable position and rested.

The storm woke her. As the rain poured down, she cupped her hands to catch some of the precious liquid. The ledge offered assistance as it collected rain in wind-eroded pockets. At least she had ample water. The afternoon heat dried her clothes, and playful breezes tousled her hair. She remained in a semiconscious state, listening to the shrill cries of red-tailed hawks teaching their young to fly. Fortunately, the mountain shaded her from the searing rays of the afternoon sun, so life was bearable, although her rock bed was beginning to feel mighty hard. That night the heavens offered a canopy of twinkling beauty for her enjoyment.

By the morning of the third day on the ledge, all the water was gone, and she was faint with hunger. "I have to find a way down," she said to herself and a little black and orange bird, which had flown to the ledge to rest. She rolled onto her uninjured side and finally got to her knees. Each movement brought stabbing pain. "Get used to it," she told herself fiercely. Her dress was in tatters. She tore a wide swatch from her petticoat and clumsily tied it around her rib cage, hoping it would help hold her together while she attempted her escape. She studied the rocky slope above her. Going that way was impossible; the rock was too loose, she would just fall again. She crept to one side of the ledge and looked down. Far below, glistening in the sunlight, was a ribbon of water. She guessed the road ran along its edge. Beyond the ledge, there was at least another hundred feet of rock before the shrubby growth began. She would have to slide down the rocks until she reached vegetation. Whimpering with fear and pain, she eased her legs over the edge of the ledge, letting her body slowly follow. She decided to slide on her back, using her legs as brakes if she started going too fast. To her surprise the rock here was more stable, and she was able to scoot herself down gradually. About ten feet from the tree line, erosion had created a small ridge, which she tumbled over, landing with a groan in a tangle of mountain laurel. Crying and shaking, she continued her descent, grabbing at bushes and small trees, stumbling over dead logs and slipping on mossy rocks. Each time she fell, her body rebelled at rising. "Stop!" it pleaded, "I'm tired! I hurt!" But Mandy pressed on.

By dusk she could hear a waterfall over to her right. She changed direction, stumbled a few hundred yards, parted the branches of a hemlock tree, and gasped with amazement. The river, which looked so tiny from the ledge, was, in reality, a wide, rocky cascade of water. She wanted to quench her demanding thirst, but the banks were steep and the water swift. Grabbing some protruding roots, she dragged her body over the bank's edge and slid into the hip-deep, icy surge. To her joy the numbing cold erased the pain of her cuts and bruises. She drank until her stomach could hold no more, then rinsed her face and arms. Now she needed rest and plenty of it.

Grabbing the roots for support, she pulled herself back up the bank and into the shelter of the hemlock. Oh, how she wished she had her satchel with its warm blanket and supplies, but it was somewhere on the mountain probably under a pile of rock. She lay on the ground, fragrant with hemlock needles, and slept.

In her exhaustive state, Mandy had failed to notice the thin, blue wisp of smoke coming from a cave just upriver. Dark eyes watched intently and noted where she lay.

Chapter Five

It was noon before she opened her eyes. For a moment she couldn't remember where she was or how she got there. She was so hungry! Her shoes were still wet with river water, so she took them off and rubbed her aching feet. Food, she had to find food. As she parted the hemlock branches and attempted to stand, a piercing pain made her gasp for breath and jogged her memory about the slide down the mountain and her broken ribs.

What was this? A small, leather pouch lay on the ground before her. Kneeling down she picked it up. It was of good leather, soft and supple. On one side a bit of beadwork formed the outline of a bird in flight. Mandy opened the pouch carefully and poured its contents into her lap. Crushed corn and dried berries! She stuffed a handful into her mouth and began to chew vigorously. Yummm! How could something so simple taste so good! Where had the pouch come from? She did not remember seeing it before. Did someone know of her whereabouts, or had it been dropped by a wayfarer? At the moment she didn't care; it was food.

"I must ration this," she said. "I'll eat only three handfuls now. Water will help fill me up." She returned the remaining mix to the pouch and pulled the strings tight, then placed the pouch under the hemlock branches. With stumbling steps she again reached the riverbank and lowered herself to the water to drink. Then she waded out to a deeper spot and let the rushing stream massage her bruised body. She endured the cold water until her teeth began to chatter then climbed onto a large, flat, sun-warmed rock to dry. After several hours her rumbling stomach roused her, and Mandy worked her way back to the tree.

Reaching under the branches for her pouch, she felt something soft. She gave a tug and out tumbled a wool blanket.

"Somebody knows I'm here," she whispered, nervously looking around. "I'll have to move on." Hurriedly she put on her shoes. Clutching the blanket and pouch she began to follow the river downstream hoping to intersect the road.

"Missy go wrong way. Path on other side of river," said a deep voice, gently. Mandy froze. A scream struggled to make its way up her throat. Suddenly an Indian, dressed in deer skin britches, appeared from behind a thicket.

"I friend. Me, Soaring Hawk." The Indian gazed at Mandy with friendly eyes. He stood quietly while she tried to decide what to do. She couldn't run; she hurt too much to fight; it was best just to yield to the circumstances.

"My name is Mandy. I guess you left me the food and blanket. Thank you. Do you have any meat? It's been so long since I've eaten meat."

"Come," said Soaring Hawk, as he turned upstream and led her to a river crossing. Mandy stumbled on a slippery rock and bent double with pain. "Missy hurt. I fix." Soaring Hawk stripped the bark off a willow tree exposing the soft inner wood. From this he cut several sections and wrapped them in moss. Continuing on, he walked away from the river, around a huge mountain laurel stand, and up a steep incline. At the top Mandy saw a cave made partly from wind erosion and partly from a granite rock outcropping. Soaring Hawk placed her blanket inside and motioned for her to enter. Stirring up the coals of a fire, he began heating water in an old blue enamel coffeepot. As the water began to simmer, he added the wood he had cut from the willow tree. Letting the brew steep until it was cool, he then gave Mandy a cupful.

"Drink. Pain go away."

Mandy took several big gulps. It had a slightly bitter taste, but wasn't too bad. Almost immediately she felt better. Lying back on her blanket, she watched Soaring Hawk move about the cave.

"I get meat," he said and silently slipped into the underbrush. Mandy stuffed another handful of the dried corn and berry mix into her mouth and washed it down with the drink the Indian had given her. Her eyes felt so heavy. She sighed gently and slept.

It was late afternoon when a light tap on her arm woke her. Soaring Hawk offered her a wooden bowl filled with a steaming, savory stew. Forgetting her manners, she gobbled it down. Patiently he filled the bowl again. This time she ate more slowly, enjoying the bits of meat, greens, and mushrooms. After the last of the delicious stew had been consumed, Soaring Hawk stepped to the back of the cave and returned carrying a tanned deerskin. "Make Indian dress," he announced, laying the hide in front of her for her approval. Mandy felt the soft leather. It was the same as the leather pouch she had found. She held the skin up to her shoulders and smiled. With a piece of charcoal, Soaring Hawk marked the seams, but it had gotten too dark in the cave to continue work on the dress so he laid it aside and left. Mandy peered out. The canopy of trees surrounding the cave was shutting out the last rays of a vibrant sunset. She could see the Indian sitting on a projecting rock, singing.

"What were you doing?" she asked when he returned.

"I thank Great Spirit for good day. Great Spirit give food. Protect Soaring Hawk."

"Oh," she replied. "You were praying. I used to say prayers when my mother was alive. I don't think God heard me, or maybe He doesn't like me. None of my prayers were answered. Ma died, and no one came to help me."

"I help," stated the Indian matter-of-factly as he lay back on his bearskin bed. Soon Mandy could hear his soft snoring blending with the many night sounds of the forest.

Mandy spent the next day eating, drinking the willow tea, and resting. Soaring Hawk had fashioned a bed by covering a thick layer of leaves and pine boughs with the hide of a black bear. Thanks to its softness and the tea, she could rest comfortably while Soaring Hawk busied himself making a squaw dress from the deerskin. It was a simple affair, the back and front were the same, and it was sewn along the sides and across the shoulders. He made the length long enough to cover her knees and fringed the bottom two inches. Next he measured her feet for a pair of moccasins. The bottoms had a thin layer of dried grasses between two soles to protect her feet from the rocky terrain. The tops came about six inches above her ankles but could be rolled down to form a soft collar.

Mandy was amazed at the Indian's survival skills. "Teach me," she pleaded. Soaring Hawk smiled.

"Missy learn Indian ways. Be safe in woods. Not go hungry."

As Soaring Hawk worked on Mandy's dress, he revealed some of his past. As a young boy, he had attended a missionary school in North Carolina. One day soldiers came and ordered the Cherokee tribe, of which he was a part, to prepare to march to a reservation. There were some skirmishes during which Soaring Hawk, several other young boys, and some older men escaped into the woods. The rest of the tribe marched all the way to Oklahoma. Thousands died along the way resulting in the journey being called the Trail of Tears.

Mandy shared with the Indian her life on the farm in Tennessee, her stepfather's brutal ways, the death of her mother, her hidey hole under the chicken coop, and her escape.

"I'm going to Pendleton, South Carolina. My cousin lives there. I'm sure she will take me in, I'm family," she declared, although in her heart she wasn't as convinced as she sounded.

"Long walk. Missy need food. Road bad. Crazy men in mountains make firewater. We take Indian path. More safe." For the next several days Soaring Hawk prepared for their journey.

Berries were picked and dried; wild meat and fish were smoked. Wild water iris tubers were dried and ground into a flour-like substance mixed with herbs and dried mushrooms. By the sixth day Mandy was somewhat re-covered. Her ribs still twinged when she twisted sideways, but otherwise she felt strong enough to resume her jour-ney.

Soaring Hawk tied a small bedroll containing a blan-ket, food, a knife, her shoes, and a wooden bowl across her back; then, shouldering a larger bundle, he led the way, following an obscure deer path. The next week was a blur of green as they hiked over shadowy mountains and into misty valleys. Mandy was amazed that Soaring Hawk moved so confidently through the maze of trees. Each morning they would eat dried meat and berries then walk until late afternoon when the Indian would select a camp-site near a stream. As Mandy prepared the fire, Soaring Hawk went in search of fresh game, always returning with wild turkey, squirrel, or fish and edible greens. The walking and natural food conditioned Mandy's body, leaving her healthier and stronger than she had ever been.

"I could almost enjoy living my whole life in the woods," she confessed one night, as she gazed at the dying embers of the campfire.

"Missy good walker. Make Indian fine wife," said Soaring Hawk with a grin.

"Not this squaw," retorted Mandy. "I have a life of my own to discover."

On the eighth day of their walk they came upon a broad, red dirt road. "Follow road toward setting sun," ordered Soaring Hawk. "Farm near. You find help."

"Is it near Pendleton?" Mandy asked, eagerly.

"Not know name. I not welcome. Trade with white man—skins for goods. He comes to woods."

Mandy smiled shyly at her Indian friend. "Thank you for taking care of me. I will remember you always."

"White girl brave as Indian. Be strong. Hard times ahead," he prophesied as he turned and disappeared into the pines.

Mandy walked as quickly as she could toward the farm. Soon a house appeared on the other side of a broad river. A ford nearby offered a shallow crossing. She could see several men working in a field. All at once she was acutely aware of her deerskin dress. "What if they think I'm a half-breed?" she wondered, remembering how people of mixed race had been tormented in her town. She stood by the side of the road uncertain of what to do. A sudden slamming of a door caused her to look to the farmhouse where a lady in a red calico dress covered by a white apron began vigorously sweeping her porch steps and stone path to the road. Mandy watched. The woman looked grandmotherly. Her graying hair was pulled back in a bun. She was stocky but muscular and plied her broom with purpose.

"Well, what is it, girl? Never seen someone sweeping before?" questioned the lady in red. "Where did you get that dress? You don't look full Indian. Speak up, or has the cat got your tongue?"

Mandy silently approached, trying to decide what to say. It seemed better to speak to this woman in a businesslike way. "Could I work for you in exchange for food and a dress like yours? I can cook and clean and do just about any outside work," she said boldly, while looking into the woman's dark brown eyes.

"Hmmm," the woman stopped sweeping and studied Mandy's slender, sinewy body. "You look strong enough to be worthwhile. I'll try you out for a day. If you don't step lively, it's out the door with ye. I've got five menfolk living here, so there's always work to be done. Come 'round back, you can start the laundry."

Mandy dutifully followed her to the back yard where a large iron pot held simmering water over a banked fire.

"I've already put in some lye soap. It should be dissolved by now. Put the whites and light colored clothes in first, a few at a time. Stir them around for a few minutes, then put them in this barrel of rinse water." She pointed to a large wooden barrel nearby. "The drying line is over yonder," she said, waving her left hand. Mandy saw a rope strung between two large oak trees near the side of the house. The mound of clothes to be washed was discouraging. She would be here most of the day under the merciless hot sun. Well, she had asked for work, so there was no use complaining. She took the stirring stick the woman held out to her and began to agitate the clothes up and down in the hot water.

"By the way, my name is Mrs. Fortune. What's yours?"

"Mandy."

"Mandy what?"

"Just Mandy. My last name isn't important."

"Hurumph! Better pick a new last name, gal, if you don't like the old one. You need a full name if you want to be respected around here."

Mandy felt like saying, "I won't be here that long," but she held her tongue. After watching her for a few minutes, Mrs. Fortune went about her business. Mandy was determined to prove her worth. She suspected Mrs. Fortune had given her the hardest job available. She stirred the soapy mess, poking the clothes to keep them under the water. After a short time, she lifted each article with her stick and dropped it into the rinse water. The sheets were so heavy she had to hold them with her hands, almost scalding herself. After a brief soak, she took each piece and inspected it for stubborn stains. For the most part the lye soap had done its job; the clothes were clean. Carefully, she hung the wash on the drying line, straightening the ends of the sheets, smoothing the pillowcases, and shaking the wrinkles out of the clothing as best she could. Because there wasn't enough line for everything, she draped the work clothes over some nearby bushes and on the back porch railing.

It was late afternoon when she finished. She was exhausted. Her deerskin dress, which had been so comfortable while she was hiking, now clung to her sweaty body like a tick on a hound dog's ear. Looking about she spotted the well pump. After a few vigorous strokes of the handle cool, clear water gushed forth. She stuck her head—hair and all—under the cooling stream. What blessed relief!

Mandy sat on the back porch steps untangling her hair so it would dry faster. She heard the back door open and footsteps approach, but she was too tired to get up.

"As long as you're sittin' you might as well do something useful." Mrs. Fortune said, passing Mandy a large pot and a knife while on her way to the small stone building halfway submerged in the earth near a huge water oak. This was the spring house where root crops, butter, meats, and other various foods were kept as cool as possible. Upon returning, she dropped a sack of potatoes at Mandy's feet.

"Peel enough to fill the pot, then put the rest back."

Mandy picked up the knife and began to peel potatoes. To combat the boredom, she thought of all the ways potatoes could be cooked. The recipes seemed endless. An hour later the pot was full, so she carried the remaining potatoes back to the spring house. As she entered the damp coolness of the stone building, she was surprised at the many shelves filled with preserves, fruits, and vegetables. Several hams hung from hooks in the ceiling, and what she guessed was bacon was wrapped in waxed paper near the door. At least the Fortune clan would not go hungry. She closed the door, picked up the pot of potatoes, and entered the kitchen.

"Set the table," ordered Mrs. Fortune without looking up from the meat she was browning in a huge iron skillet. "Silver in the top drawer, plates in the cupboard."

Mandy remembered how she had been shown to set the table at the boarding house. Spoons here, forks there. She didn't know whether to include herself or not, but set an extra place just in case. The sky was streaked with evening clouds when the men came clomping up the back steps.

"I'm hungry, ma! What's for dinner?" shouted one burly fellow in a sweat-stained shirt as he entered the kitchen. Seeing Mandy, he stopped short. "Looks like ma finally got her wish; a gal to help with the chores, and a pretty one at that. Now ma'll probably get all gussied up and visit the parson's wife for tea everyday."

A chorus of guffaws followed as the other fellows curiously stared at Mandy, who pretended not to notice.

As quickly and secretly as she could she removed the extra place setting from the dining room table. She would feel more comfortable eating in the kitchen away from the probing eyes of Mrs. Fortune's brood.

Everyday for the next week Mandy worked from dawn to dusk. The house had to be cleaned and scrubbed, meals prepared, clothes washed, and the garden weeded. Sunday arrived and with it came a welcome day of rest. In spite of their boisterous ways and backbreaking labor at the sawmill and farm, the Fortune family attended church whenever possible. After the habitual Saturday night baths, clean suits were laid out for each member of the family in anticipation of Sunday services. Mandy found herself in possession of a black gabardine dress, which she suspected Mrs. Fortune had outgrown years before. It smelled musty, and there was dust in its folds. She hated it. To combat the smell, she brushed it thoroughly and hung it on the drying line to air. The color was depressing, the material was too hot for summer, and it fit like a sack, but at least she was dressed in civilized clothing. She had not left the house or yard since she had arrived, so no one except the Fortune family had seen her in Indian garb.

The church was located about a half-mile away from the house. Mandy thought it looked to be an abandoned log barn that had been reclaimed. Services were held only when a circuit riding preacher or lay pastor came to the area.

Mrs. Fortune and her sons walked to church, displaying unusual dignity as they greeted other families parking their wagons in the churchyard. Mandy brought up the rear, staying as far back as possible.

The sermon was about sin and its reward: death and hell. She shivered as the detailed scene of tortured souls, crying for relief was painted verbally in her mind. What kind of God would delight in torturing people? Is that how her life would end? She decided to ignore God for the moment. Death seemed to her a distant future event. Perhaps He would have a change of heart before she had to face Him.

Sunday dinner had been prepared on Saturday. Mrs. Fortune did not believe in working on the Sabbath, proclaiming it a day of visiting and relaxation. As Mandy washed the dishes, she could hear the voices of visitors in the parlor. The men either went courting or gathered outside to discuss crops, the weather, or livestock. The women had tea and cakes inside and talked about babies, fashions, and recipes.

Again, the familiar ache rose inside her as she realized she was the outsider. There was no warmth in the Fortune family. They made no effort to make her feel like anything but a servant. Their milk of human kindness had soured. For all their religious ways, they were still proud and self-absorbed. It was time to leave. Mandy decided to ask Mrs. Fortune for wages or traveling supplies. She had worked diligently for a week. Perhaps her reward would be a pair of shoes along with food and some personal items.

The next day Mrs. Fortune was confined to her bed with a "skull splitting headache" as she described it. Mandy was told to work in the kitchen garden and not bother anyone. Here was her golden opportunity to find out how far it was to Pendleton. She pretended to be weeding as she watched for a passing wagon to slow for the ford crossing. Finally her patience was rewarded as a man and woman in a buckboard drove by. She hurried to the road to meet them and asked, "Have you ever heard of Pendleton, South Carolina?"

"Pendleton is well known to me. I get fresh cotton seed oil from there. It takes a full day by buggy; the road is good, but there are several dangerous mountain curves to maneuver," remarked the man.

"Are you going there soon?" inquired Mandy, hopefully.

"No. It will be several months yet before the cotton seeds are pressed."

Mandy's heart sank. She had hoped for a ride. Several months would be too long to wait. "Which way do you go?"

"I follow the road by the grist mill. It goes within five miles of Pendleton."

"Are you living with the Fortune family?" asked the lady.

"No, I am just working here for a short time to earn some money. I'm on my way to Pendleton"

"Has Mrs. Fortune paid you anything yet?"

"No, but I suspect she will give me a wage this week."

"It will be the first time," the man replied with a rueful laugh. " That old lady has every penny her boys ever earned. I heard she's saving for her funeral. Wants it to be the fanciest the folks around here have ever seen. Imagine skimping on living in order to die in style. There's no understanding some folks." With a shake of his head, he clucked to his team and slowly approached the river as his wife gave Mandy a wave good-by.

Mandy was dismayed by the man's assessment of her employer. So the dress she was given was her wages for the week. It was mighty poor pay for all the hard work she had done. Well, she knew the way to Pendleton now, so what was she waiting for?

When she returned to the house, Mrs. Fortune was still sleeping. Hurriedly, Mandy gathered some left over biscuits, took an old shawl hanging on a hook by the back door to wrap her deer skin dress in, and went to the spring house. Into the shawl also went a huge hunk of ham, some potatoes, carrots, and several jars of preserves. She tried to take enough food for four days. After putting on her moccasins (which she had not worn since she had been given the black dress), she planned her route. By keeping to the back orchard until she was away from the farmhouse, she could cross over to the grist mill road. When she finally was safely in the shadows of the mountain forest, she took off the black dress and put on her soft deerskin. She felt better already. Pendleton was only a few days away. She would make it after all.

Chapter Six

The final stages of her trip were rather uneventful. The road was easy to follow, just one hairpin turn after another. The first two days were exhausting, but then the road seemed to straighten out and gently meander downward. Once she left the mountains, the land became a patchwork of cotton, corn, and grain fields. Mandy tried to remain as inconspicuous as possible, especially when a wagon or horse and rider passed. On the fourth day, because of the traffic, she decided it was better to travel in the very early morning and again at twilight. The moon was full, so she could see well enough to follow the road at night. In spite of her careful rationing, her food was soon gone. One night she found a large garden near the road and surreptitiously filled her shawl with yellow squash and green beans.

By noon the next day, she could tell she was nearing a town, so she hid behind some sumac bushes and put on her black gabardine dress. She wanted to make a good impression. Finding a creek, she washed her face and hands, then smoothed her hair. Holding herself stiffly erect, she marched into the hustle and bustle of buggies, farm wagons, and pedestrians. To her amazement, the people paid her no attention. After walking several blocks, she spied a young gentleman loading a wagon with farm supplies. He looked harmless enough, but she approached him with caution.

"Excuse me, sir, I am looking for the road to Pendleton."

"You're standing on it. Follow this for five miles and you'll be in the center of Pendleton," he replied.

"Thank you." Mandy started to walk away.

"If you'll wait 'til I'm loaded, I'll give you a ride. My wife is at the general store yonder," he said, pointing across the street. "My name is John Clancy."

"I'm Mandy." So saying, she sat down on the wagon tongue. It would look much better to arrive in Pendleton in the company of neighbors than to walk in alone. She felt safe knowing the man's wife was with him.

After a few minutes, a simply dressed woman appeared at the back of the wagon with several bundles. Placing them in one corner, she then stood in the shade nearby. Mandy walked over to her.

"Mrs. Clancy? My name is Mandy. Your husband said it would be all right if I rode with you to Pendleton."

"If John invited you I'm happy to have you ride along." Mrs. Clancy said in a low, musical voice. "Do you live in Pendleton?"

"I hope to. My cousin spends the summers there. I'm here for a visit."

"What's your cousin's name? Perhaps I know her."

"Cornelia Drake. She really lives in Charleston but the whole family comes to Pendleton for the summer."

"Ah, yes. There are many families from the Low Country, who have summer homes in this district in order to avoid the summer sickness that rages through the coastal area. I do not personally know the Drakes, but I have heard their name mentioned. I'm sure you will have no trouble finding them." She smiled at Mandy then turned toward her husband, who was carrying a wooden box which he dropped with a thud into the back of the wagon.

"That's all the hardware," he said, as he helped his wife and Mandy onto the wagon's wooden seat. "I have to stop at the lumber yard, then we are on our way."

By mid-afternoon Mandy found herself bumping along a red dirt road on the last few miles of her journey. As the wagon rumbled across a stone bridge and up a gentle slope, the first building to fill Mandy's sight was a new two-story general store.

"This store will be open in another month or two," said Mrs. Clancy. " Then we will be able to buy just about anything we need just a few miles from home. Of course, we have several other fine shops, but this one will carry the most variety."

Mandy was impressed with its size. It looked large enough to be a hotel. Across the street, she saw a beautiful columned rectangular building set amid towering oaks and a grassy lawn.

Mr. Clancy followed her gaze. "That is the Farmers' Society Hall. The first floor is used as the post office; the second story is the meeting hall."

Mandy felt an immediate affinity with Pendleton. The tidy little shops surrounding the Farmers' Hall formed a square with a wide road running in between. Beyond the business district large houses overlooked the square, and everywhere beautiful shade trees and flowering shrubs offered coolness and fragrance.

As Mr. Clancy stopped the horses at the watering trough to refresh themselves, Mrs. Clancy chatted with several passing women.

"This is a friendly town and very progressive. I'm sure you will be happy here. Most of the Low Country folk live about a mile in that direction, unless they are operating plantations. If you ask at the pharmacy over there, I'm certain you will find your cousin."

Mandy thanked the Clancys and jumped from the wagon. She was anxious to get settled, so she went directly to the building Mrs. Clancy had singled out.

A stocky man in a short, white coat peered at her over wire-rimmed glasses.

"Could you tell me where Cornelia Drake lives, please?"

"The old Drake house is down the road that runs behind this building. Turn left; then go about three miles. Look for a large house behind a stone wall."

Three miles! It seemed she wasn't through walking yet. Thanking the pharmacist, Mandy walked in the direction he had indicated. They must have a large farm, she thought as she passed fields of corn. The sun was beating down on her head, making her thirsty. Each time a wagon passed the red dust of the road blew up in clouds that threatened to choke her. A thousand thoughts raced through her mind, but her greatest concern was being accepted as a relative. Had her mother ever written to her cousin in recent years? She really had no proof of her family ties other than the fact she looked much like her ma. She tried to recall everything she had heard about her family, but realized she knew very little.

After an hour of trudging through the dust, Mandy saw the stone wall complete with a wrought-iron gate. She gave the gate a mighty push and stood facing a large house with a wraparound porch surrounded by huge water oaks. It seemed unusually quiet. Perhaps everyone was in town or having a nap. Cautiously, she climbed the front steps and knocked on the door. After a few minutes the door opened a crack, revealing unfriendly, dark eyes.

"Good afternoon," Mandy said, politely. "Is Cornelia Drake at home? My name is Mandy. I've come for a visit."

"She ain't here," said a soft voice. "She and her family dun gone to New Jersey."

"New Jersey?" Mandy's voice faltered with despair. "When will she be back?"

"Ain't goin' to come back here. This house is sold. I'se gettin' it ready for new peoples."

"Not coming back. . . ." Mandy's mind reeled with disappointment and fear. Suddenly a deep blackness enveloped her, and she fell with a crash to the porch floor.

Chapter Seven

When Mandy opened her eyes, she saw a room full of flowers winding their way over painted ribbons of blue. It was the prettiest wallpaper she had ever seen. She was lying in a trundle bed, her feet hanging out the bottom, and her arms brushing the floor. She spent a moment trying to remember where she was. Oh, yes. The Drake summer house, but without the Drakes. Now what should she do? Where could she go? One thing for certain, she was not going back to Tennessee! Thoughts hammered at her brain, giving her a tension headache. She sat up and looked around. Dust covers obscured the scanty bit of remaining furniture, and with the shades drawn the room resembled a tomb. Hastily she got up, opened the door, and stepped out into the hall. The smell of food cooking made her mouth water and her stomach growl. She followed the tantalizing odors.

"Wal, chile, hep yer sef," said the same voice that spoke to her when she arrived. "You is all skin an' bones. Whereveh you is from, mos' likely food was scarcer n' hens' teeth."

Mandy gazed at the biscuits, greens, and ham hock. She filled a plate then sat on the back porch steps and concentrated on the feast. Fear fled as her stomach filled. She wiped her mouth with the back of her hand and passed her empty plate to the black lady gently rocking in the porch rocker.

"That was mighty good. Thank you."

"My name is Goldie," replied the woman. "I live out yondah, but Mistah Drake hired me to clean out the house."

"Maybe I could stay here and help? Do you think the new family will need a maid?" Mandy suggested in quiet desperation as she nervously fingered the silver cross around her neck.

"I ain't bein' responsible for no stranger in this house, no way, no how," Goldie said, firmly. "Y'all kin stay til I leaves, then you goes, too."

"I don't have any place to go. I was planning to stay with my cousin. I don't know anybody else in Pendleton."

"Wal, you gots two days to git acquainted. Go into town tomorrow and ask around. Mebbe somebodies there need help. Best now if you rest yo' weary bones." Goldie walked toward the outhouse, ending the conversation.

Mandy sat in the rocking chair Goldie had vacated. "All this way for nothing!" she said to herself, as she slowly rocked. The motion and the full meal made her sleepy, and she dozed in the chair. The next thing she knew Goldie was shaking her.

"Time for bed. You kin sleep on the porch or in the back room where you was," she said.

Still half asleep, Mandy shuffled back to the trundle bed. Then she realized, she needed a trip to the outhouse, so she stumbled back down the hall and out the back door. The 'necessary' was off to the side yard behind some bushes. It was almost dark. She hoped Goldie had taken the time to clean and air it. She hated fighting spiders and bees while relieving herself. To her joy, she found it quite respectable. Since it had been unused for a while, it was almost odor free. She found a small barrel of rainwater and a bar of soap nearby. A wash-up made her feel refreshed and relaxed. She decided tomorrow she would wash her clothes and take a bath. If she was to look for work, she needed to be as presentable as possible.

Morning was half gone when Mandy awoke. She slipped on her chemise and wandered to the outside kitchen in search of Goldie. The building was empty, but a large bowl of grits and gravy sat on the counter next to a spoon. She assumed they were for her and proceeded to make short work of her breakfast. Next, she gathered up her clothes, wrapping a sheet from her bed around her to cover her nakedness and proceeded to the barrel by the outhouse where she scrubbed every item she owned. She hung her clothes over a drying line and went in search of some warm water for a bath just as Goldie appeared in the doorway.

"They's some warm water on the stove in a bucket. You kin wash up in there, too. They's extra buckets under the sink, but no tub large enough for sittin'."

Mandy was disappointed. She had really wanted to soak for a while, but she did the best she could and felt better. She couldn't stand having dirty hair.

Goldie returned with several coverlets in her arms. "Lucky it's bin a dry year," she commented. "Not much mildew to fuss with. Ol' man sun will kill dese germs quick enough." With a twist of her arm she flung the coverlets on the line next to Mandy's clothing. "Long as you is here, you kin hep me air the drapes."

Mandy followed her into a large formal sitting room, where green damask drapes hung from gilded wooden poles.

"Not many fancies in this house. Most windows have jist shutters so to let in the cool night air. But Miz Drake, she liked this room to be proud," remarked Goldie.

A wave of sadness engulfed Mandy, as she stood in

the empty room and realized she would not be enjoying
the summer with family. Then she had an idea. "Goldie,
are there other families here that will be returning to
Charleston in the fall? Perhaps I could travel with one of
them and try to find other relatives. "

"Mebbe, but don' count on it. Charleston peoples is
mighty close. They don't cotton to taking in strangers.
'Sides, you don't even talk right. You needs teachin', gots
to learn genteel ways an' slow talk. You act like you is
fresh off de farm."

Mandy inwardly bristled. She hadn't noticed any major
differences between her and the folks she had met. If
anybody needed speech lessons it was Goldie. Then she
looked at the black gabardine dress, swaying in the breeze
and laughed. What a sight she must have been wearing a
dress several sizes too large and long since out of style.
Goldie was right; she would stick out like a sore thumb
in any social gathering.

"I need a dress, Goldie, one that fits. Did the Drakes
leave a chest of discards?"

"They's a trunk of rags in the attic. See if they be
anything useful."

Mandy climbed the rickety steps into the stuffy attic.
She could see the trunk in a corner. Opening it she found
a green gingham dress and a rose crocheted shawl. After
rummaging deeper, she came across faded petticoats and
bloomers. An old straw hat with a wide brim trimmed
with ragged flowers hung on a peg. She gathered up everything she thought would be usable and climbed down.

It was fun trying everything on. Goldie agreed the
green dress looked the best and offered to alter it to fit
Mandy's boyish figure. The hat was cleaned and a piece
of the scrap material from the green dress made a pretty
sash to tie around the band. By late afternoon everything
had been reworked, washed, and dried in the summer

breeze. Mandy pulled her hair back with a piece of ribbon she had found and put on a pair of fancy slippers (with just a little hole in the sole) she had rescued from the trunk. The total effect was quite pleasing. She looked like a budding lady.

"I'm off to town, Goldie. Wish me luck." The afternoon heat had driven most shoppers home to sit on their shady porches. Mandy strolled along the square looking in the shop windows. The store with books displayed in the window looked interesting, so she stepped inside.

"Good afternoon, Miss. Looking for something special?" asked a high tenor voice.

Mandy cleared her throat and straightened her shoulders. "Yes, I am. I need to find work. Would you know of any job suitable for me? I can do all kinds of housework; I even helped in a boarding house for a while."

"Bless my soul," said the man softly, as he studied the thin, but determined face before him. "I need to think on this a bit; a cup of tea always helps clear my mind. Would you care to join me? Clayton McAbee is the name."

Mandy accepted his offer. She had just walked three miles in the blazing sun and was very thirsty. She would have preferred cold water, but she didn't want to seen rude. Mr. McAbee arranged a plate with some shortbread cookies, then produced two steaming cups of tea. They sat on a bench that Mr. McAbee cleared of bookbindings.

"I've been here seven years, but I still have my tea in the afternoon. What's good for a Scot in Aberdeen is good for a Scot in Pendleton," he said. Mandy listened as he relived his voyage from Scotland to America. He had settled in Pendleton because of the number of Scottish families in the area. Some, of his clan, were considered distant relatives. He had tried his hand at farming, but the heat was too much for a man from a city in northern Scotland, where the summer twilight lasted until the wee hours of the morning. Printing and bookbinding were his forte, and he managed a nice life on their profits.

"I've an instinct for the books people want to read, and now with the industrialization issue there are handbills passed around almost daily. Besides, I print a weekly newspaper. You've come to the right person; I have a finger on the pulse of Pendleton. I'm the first to know of new businesses and new families in the area. Sakes alive! I've just had a fetching thought! The Woodburn plantation has a new owner. A man of the cloth, Dr. John Adger, I believe is his name. A missionary whose failing eyesight caused him to leave his post and move here. I heard tell just the other day he was looking for household help. What with his poor eyesight and all, perhaps he'll not notice your young age." Mr. McAbee smiled encouragingly.

Mandy's heart beat faster. A plantation! Fresh air and land instead of stuffy rooms and steamy kitchens. "How do I get there?" she asked, hurriedly sipping the last of her tea.

The plantation was an easy mile walk. The large, two story white clapboard with tall windows and massive square columns supporting double porches was tucked amid huge shady oaks of several varieties—water oaks with small fluted leaves and white oaks that stretched their branches and broad leaves over the wraparound porch. Even from a distance the house looked impressive. A white picket fence enclosed a grassy yard that contained a carriage house and storage shed.

As Mandy approached, she couldn't decide whether to climb the steps to the front door or go around back to the servant's entry. She concluded she looked presentable enough for the front, besides, perhaps the missionary himself would greet her. She didn't want to talk to any hired help.

With head erect, she proceeded to the front porch steps. She could hear a booming voice reciting aloud on the far side of the porch. Curious, she peered around the corner. In a rocker, a man of medium build with a bushy brown beard and closely cropped hair was speaking to himself, or so Mandy thought. When he paused for a moment, she stepped forward.

"Excuse me. . . ."

"Quiet, please. I'm in the midst of conversing with the Almighty. Take a seat, I'll be done shortly."

Embarrassed, Mandy walked out of earshot. The view from the porch included rolling pastureland and majestic woods. A red clay buggy road ran in front of the pasture. It did not seen to be heavily traveled, as there was the usual center strip of grass between the two wheel ruts. From a nearby hydrangea bush a mockingbird sang a borrowed song, and in the background Mandy could hear the clank of pots and pans.

Perhaps she was too late; maybe the positions had been filled. Someone was working in the kitchen, and it was evident a gardener had been busy trimming the growth around the house. "Hurry up and finish!" she said in a whisper as she waved a buzzing gnat away from her eyes. She hated waiting.

"All right, miss. You may return now and state your business," the booming voice called. Mandy smoothed her dress and walked, with what she hoped passed for self-assurance, to the side porch. A cool breeze swept across her forehead as she stood before the gentleman.

"My name is Mandy. Mr. McAbee from the book store suggested I see you about working on your plantation," she said as politely and positively as she could. "I am honest, capable, and experienced in gardening, cooking, and general housework." She hesitated. How much should she tell? Would the missionary feel sorry for her if she explained her plight? Perhaps he would think her foolish or irresponsible for leaving the farm. She decided not to mention her past, but to ask for lodging. "I will need a place to stay, but just a small room with a cot will be fine." She stood quietly, waiting for his reply.

"You aren't from these parts, are you?"

"No, sir."

"Do you have any references?"

"No, sir. I came to Pendleton looking for my cousin, Cornelia Drake, but she has moved away. I need a place to stay, until I can make other arrangements."

"Ah, yes. The Charleston Drakes. Quite a family. I take it she was not informed you were coming?"

"No, sir."

"Well, now. You are in quite a predicament. Can you grow vegetables?" Dr. Adger asked, in a kindly voice.

"Yes, sir. And tend chickens and milk goats. I also worked at a boarding house for a time and learned to cook and serve. I'm thin but strong, and I don't eat much. You'll never know I'm around except when I'm doing household chores. I'm neat and clean and would be no bother." Suddenly the words seem to rush out of her mouth in anticipation of a safe haven.

"I will be able to pay you just a small salary besides your room and board. Due to my poor eyesight, I am not able at this time to accept a parish or a teaching position, so my assets are limited. I spent twelve years as a missionary in Armenia—originally called Ararat—where Noah's ark rested after the flood, you know. What a trip that was! Sixty-four days on a tiny brig called the Padang. My wife was seasick all the way. I translated the New Testament and Bible tracts into the language of the people. My wife and I lost our first three children due to the barbaric conditions there. Fortunately, the Almighty saw fit to give us more offspring once we returned to Charleston.

The past five years, I have spent preaching and teaching the Negroes in that fine city. They are almost as ignorant of the scriptures as the Armenians. But my eyes are so strained now that reading or writing is nigh on impossible."

Mandy nodded. They were somewhat in the same situation: strangers in a strange town living under adverse circumstances.

When Dr. Adger finished reminiscing, he sat in silence for a few minutes, then turned to Mandy. "I've told you my story, now you tell me yours."

Mandy briefly sketched her life on the farm, her happy days with her mother and father, the abuse of her stepfather, the death of her mother, and her walk to Pendleton. She put on a courageous front, pretending not to be in distress at her homeless situation.

"You've had a full life already," commented Dr. Adger. "The Almighty must have a special plan for you to have brought you safely thus far."

Mandy ignored the observation. If God had been the instigator of all her troubles, she was better off not becoming too friendly with Him. So far, the only person who had shown much Christian charity had been Soaring Hawk, who practiced Indian tribal beliefs and was considered a heathen by society. The so-called Christians she had met proved themselves to be worldly-minded, greedy, legalistic penny-pinchers. There was nothing in their religion that appealed to her.

Dr. Adger rose to his feet and carefully shuffled toward the main door. "Let me fetch Mrs. Whitehall who oversees the household help. She can decide where to put you and what duties to assign you. I am here to recover, God willing, and I intend to eat a healthy diet. A vegetable garden that produces a large variety of produce year 'round is my first priority. It's almost time to plant the fall greens. The soil must be prepared. I have a man to do the heavy work, but I'm sure Mrs. Whitehall will be delighted to turn over the planting and maintenance responsibilities to you. She detests outside work. Afraid of aging her skin, I think. Such vanity!"

Mandy remembered how carefully her mother had shaded her face with a large sun bonnet and also kept her hands soft by coating them with lard, when she worked in the soil. A lump rose in Mandy's throat. Oh! If she could only feel her ma's soft hands stroking her forehead just once more! She forced the lump back down into her stomach and followed Dr. Adger inside.

Mandy's poise returned as she stood in the parlor. The rooms were large with fourteen-foot ceilings and windows that almost reached the full height. There was a noticeable absence of halls; each room seemed to flow into the next. The fireplace in the parlor had an ornate mantel and Italian tiles along its sides. There were vases of flowers on mahogany tables; the furniture was well used, but tasteful. The many windows let in the outdoor light, creating a bright, airy decor. Dr. Adger called his wife, who greeted Mandy shyly, wished her well, deferred to her husband's decision, and then disappeared in the direction of the nursery to attend their four small children.

When Mrs. Whitehall heard Mandy was to help with the garden she welcomed her with open arms. "I've enough just keeping the house clean and picking up after the family without killing myself in an everlasting battle with weeds and varmits," she said as she led Mandy down to a cellar room that had a cot and a chair. "It's a bit dank in the winter, but you'll enjoy the cool and quiet the rest of the year. The kitchen is off to the right. You can use the small sink for wash ups. If you walk through that door, you'll be a stone's throw from the garden," she said, pointing to large double doors that opened onto a brick patio.

The land at the back of the house sloped so the basement opened out to the back yard. Beyond the clearing Mandy could see another plantation house on a distant hill, overlooking cultivated fields stretching in every direction. It was an altogether pleasing sight, making her sigh with pleasure. Even without the security of family, Pendleton looked promising.

Chapter Eight

Mandy's life soon developed a rhythm of its own. Up at dawn, a breakfast of biscuits and honey or grits and seasonal fruit. Then, she worked in the garden until two o'clock when the main meal was served. Dr. Adger did, indeed, enjoy healthy food. There were always several vegetables and fruits on the menu plus corn bread or whole wheat buns, stews, custards, and lemonade. Mrs. Whitehall was as excellent cook. The meal was eaten slowly and each person was encouraged to contribute to the constant conversation. All the household help ate at the same table with the missionary, an unusual custom for those days, but one of which Mandy approved. By so doing, everyone knew what was going on and what the needs of the plantation were. Mrs. Adger usually ate her main meal with the children at an earlier hour.

The rest of her day was spent helping Mrs. Whitehall can or dry the garden's bounty. Soon, the shelves in the large basement pantry were laden with colorful rows of corn relish, canned vegetables, berries, fruit jams, and jellies, dried beans, black-eyed peas, and pickled concoctions that would defy the imagination. One of Mandy's favorite fruits was the wild persimmon that ripened to a rusty orange after the first frost. Persimmon trees grew wild in patches throughout the plantation. Mrs. Whitehall sieved the fruit to remove the large, black seeds and bitter skin then made puddings or muffins with the pulp. Mandy enjoyed eating the fruit right off the tree, spitting the seeds as far as she could at some imaginary target. An unripe persimmon would turn to bitter grit in her mouth, making her face screw up in agony. She would spit until she had no more saliva left, trying to get every morsel of the unripe fruit from around her teeth and out of her mouth.

The nutritious food soon worked its healing powers in Dr. Adger. His eyesight improved and his skin's pallor changed to a healthy glow. The better he felt, the more sociable he became. One day he announced plans to hold a Christmas open house for friends and neighbors. Pendleton was a town of many social gatherings, and he felt it time to contribute to its gaiety. Mrs. Whitehall turned to Mandy with a grimace. She had hoped for an easy holiday season, but an open house demanded an abundance of seasonal decorations and a banquet table groaning with food.

The day of the party Mandy was sent to gather boughs of holly, cedar, pine, and magnolia. The red camellia blossoms and the grape-like clusters of red nandina berries added holiday color to the greens which were placed on mantles, tables, and window ledges. Bayberry scented candles burned brightly in every room. The dining table offered a myriad of culinary delights including fruitcakes, tarts, cream and fruit pies, vegetable casseroles, hams, wild turkey, and spicy fruit compotes. On the sideboard rested a huge bowl of eggnog, accompanied by bottles of whiskey and rum, so the gentlemen could flavor the drink according to their tastes. Fires burned brightly in all the fireplaces, and several musicians played Christmas carols on their violins.

Mandy, in a new red wool dress given to her as a present by the Adgers and Mrs. Whitehall, was as proud of the plantation as if it were her own. She stood in the dining room ready to assist anyone who needed help carrying refreshments to a chair or table. Seeing the ladies and young girls in their fashionable gowns stimulated latent desires to meet local girls of her own age. She knew some of them because they attended the same church she did. (Dr. Adger insisted all his help go to church at least once a week.) She decided to ask if she could attend the weekly youth gatherings at a nearby house of worship, which consisted of ordinary farm folk and not the Low Country aristocrats.

It was past midnight when the last guest departed. Fortunately, the weather was almost balmy, so there would be no frost-nipped fingers or toes. Mandy stood on the porch breathing in the sharp smell of the pines. Countless stars glittered in the heavens, while tree frogs croaked their own melodies of peace and good will. Dr. Adger joined her, gazing at the night sky.

"On a night like this our Savior was born in a crude stable, with animals and shepherds to tell of His birth. An ignoble beginning to God's plan for the ages. Now we proclaim Christ King of kings and Lord of lords. Never underestimate the power of God, Mandy. With Him nothing is impossible," he said.

That night as Mandy slept the sleep of an exhausted young girl, the words "with Him nothing is impossible" echoed over and over in her mind, as the familiar dream of the house with the wrought iron gate played itself out in her subconscious.

One cold, rainy January day Dr. Adger called to Mandy. "You have a pleasant voice. Would you read some passages of Scripture to me? My vision does not yet allow serious reading."

Mandy stared at the floor, shuffling her feet. "I can't read," she said softly, her face scarlet with shame.

"Can't read? Why ever not? Have you had no schooling?"

"My pa died just when ma was teaching me the alphabet. My step-pa didn't hold with educating girls. He said God meant them for childbearing and field work."

"Such nonsense! He had a twisted understanding of Scripture. God gave both men and women brains, and He expects us to use them to honor Him. Sit right down and we'll start your reading lessons."

So began Mandy's education. For an hour each day she recited the alphabet, read out loud, and practiced writing. It wasn't long before she could sound out almost any word she did not recognize and could read simple books out loud without stumbling. Dr. Adger was delighted with her progress and added arithmetic, Latin, and geography to her lessons.

Spring came early that year. It was common to see the happy, bobbing, yellow heads of daffodils in February, but by mid-March the countryside was ablaze with the blossoms of red bud trees, white dogwood, pink azaleas, and yellow scotch broom. Mandy spent her days on hands and knees planting beets, lettuce, peas, carrots, Swiss chard, and other spring crops. The clear, crisp air of winter had given way to the warm, humid vapors of spring.

"It's a miracle!" proclaimed Dr. Adger one morning, as he stood gazing over the misty pastures. "I can see almost as well as I could before my missionary appointment. The good Lord is giving me another opportunity for active service. I must look for a parish or boys' school that needs my abilities." Mandy was glad the Reverend's eyesight had improved, but was worried as to what would become of her if he moved away. She had become attached to Woodburn and thought of Dr. Adger as a benevolent uncle.

Several weeks later, Dr. Adger called Mandy into his study. "I have been offered a co-professorship position at a seminary in Columbia this coming fall and have sold Woodburn to my brother. Life here will change, and I don't think you will be needed as you now are. Besides, you are growing into a fine young lady and should enjoy the company of your peers along with the social instruction so necessary for acceptance among Low Country families. I have talked to Dr. Gibbes, and he assures me his family would be delighted to have you live with them until you can find your way clear to continue your search for your relatives. You already know his two daughters by sight, Clarissa and Annabelle. They attend the Old Stone Church and sit just two rows ahead of us. They have promised to see to your education and train you in the necessary customs. It's a wonderful opportunity for you. I'll not abandon you; I'll give you an address where you may contact me if things go amiss, but truly I believe the hand of God is in this."

Mandy did recall seeing the Gibbes girls, but had not actually talked to them. She was too shy to mingle with aristocratic families. She felt more comfortable with the local farm youths who did an honest day's work and lived simpler lives. Still, Dr. Adger had gone to great lengths to provide for her, and she must be grateful. As Goldie had told her, she needed to learn genteel ways, but would she ever have a place she could call home? She had scarcely settled in, and now she was on the move again!

Promptly at four o'clock the following Wednesday, Dr. Adger pulled the bell tassel at The Glen, the home of Dr. Arthur Gibbes and his wife, Phoebe. It was a large two-story house with the typical wide columned wrap-around porch loved by Low Country people. The Glen was located on Friendville property, which was the name of the plantation owned by the Stuarts, Phoebe's adopted parents. This whole section of Pendleton was referred to as the Low Country settlement. All the houses sat a good distance from the road and had gates opening onto the grounds. It was an area of tall trees, beautiful gardens, and culture where the ladies served tea on their porches (called piazzas) in the afternoon, and large parlors were opened often for formal dinner-dances that lasted well into the night. At Dr. Adger's second pull the large ornate door was slowly opened by a black man, dressed in the formal attire of the house butler.

"Would you please tell Mrs. Gibbes that Dr. Adger and Miss Mandy are calling," said The Reverend as they were ushered into a large, formal hall.

"Dr. Adger! How kind of you to come!" chirped a vivacious woman dressed in a blue-grey cotton sateen dress overlaid with cream lace. Her dark auburn hair was pulled back and held in a cream lace hair net. She had large, flashing eyes that were the same color as the dress which accentuated her peaches and cream complexion. With a graceful turn that set her hooped dress swaying, she led them into the front formal parlor where a carved walnut table held the tea tray, and fine bone china dishes were filled with tantalizing desserts.

"Do sit down and help yourselves to these lovely tarts," she said as she regally seated herself at one end of the table and proceeded to pour out the tea. "Miss Mandy, we have heard your brave tale of adventure from Rev. Adger. Dr. Gibbes and I will be only too happy to add you to our family. I must warn you, however, that our daughters will no doubt make life a bit challenging for you. They tease each other mercilessly, and you will not be exempt. Do you have the fortitude to endure such behavior?"

"I hope so, ma'am. I'm very thankful for your interest in my situation," replied Mandy. "I will do my best not to be a bother. I expect to contact a family member soon, so I will not be a burden to you for very long."

"I'm sure you will not be a burden at all. It is our
Christian duty to look after widows and orphans. We
count it a privilege to welcome you to our home." Mrs.
Gibbes flashed Mandy a warm smile, as she lifted her
teacup to her mouth.

Several hours later, all the arrangements had been
made. Mandy was to live with the Gibbes, who would be
responsible for her upbringing. The fact that she claimed
to be related to the Charleston Drakes played no little
part in their decision. So when Dr. Adger packed his
belongings in anticipation of the teaching position in
Columbia, Mandy gathered her possessions and moved
into another chapter of her life.

Chapter Nine

Living at the Gibbes was like entering another world. For the first week Mandy tried to blend in with the woodwork. She was embarrassed about her plain, outdated dresses, and backwoods ways. She watched the girls spend hours fussing over their appearance. Each curl of their hair had to be the exact same length; every ruffle on their dresses had to lie just so. Their giggling, simpering, and exaggerated emotions set Mandy's nerves on edge.

"Mama, Mandy needs a dress with a hoop," said Clarissa one morning, as she watched Mandy approach the breakfast table. "If she isn't properly attired she will never fit in. Have Ruby remake my lavender batiste. The color never did suit me."

"Mandy needs more than stylish clothes to become a Low Country debutante," replied Mrs. Gibbes. "Why don't you girls teach her Southern manners? I'm sure she will feel much more comfortable with your friends, if she knows our customs. Bring me your dress, Clarissa, I'll have Ruby remake it today. You'd best teach Mandy how to handle a hoop. Remember the struggle you had learning to sit."

Clarissa laughed. "Annabelle, we've got a summer project. We are going to make a silk purse out of this sow's ear! No offense, Mandy. It will be fun! Really! You already have good posture. All we have to do is teach you the finer points of being a southern lady."

A tiny smile flickered across Mandy's face. A southern lady, indeed! Well, it would probably be easier learning to simper and curtsy than working in the Pendleton cloth factory or being a cook in one of the hotels. She had to admit the Gibbes were very considerate of her. She was almost treated as one of the family, so she certainly didn't want to be the source of any embarrassment. "When do we start?" she asked, determined to become the best the South had to offer.

The Gibbes were a religious family. Mrs. Gibbes presided over morning devotions as soon as breakfast was finished. Each girl recited a scripture by memory and explained its meaning. Passages from the Psalms and Gospels were read, then came prayer. With her eyes tightly shut, Mandy asked God to help her learn Low Country customs quickly. She wasn't sure how long she could stand Clarissa and Annabelle lording over her. With devotions ended, the girls rushed Mandy upstairs. They quickly assembled a hoop frame, which they dropped over Mandy's head and tied tightly around her waist. The whalebone hoop banged uncomfortably against her ankles.

"Walk like this," commanded Clarissa, hoisting her skirt above her shins to show Mandy the short, gliding steps that made the hoop sway gently from side to side. Mandy took a few tentative steps. Whoomp! The hoop crashed against her legs. With each step it built momentum until it was swinging in wild gyrations.

Annabelle bent double with laughter. "We ought to hook her to the churn. We'd have fresh buttermilk in no time."

Clarissa, walking slowly with an exaggerated rhythm, paraded in front of Mandy. "Recite a poem or hymn to keep a steady pace. 'Amazing grace, how sweet the sound . . .' Head up, shoulders back, step, step."

Mandy grabbed the hoop supports to stabilize them and watched Clarissa. Small steps; flexed knees. She tried again, counting to herself. This time the hoop rocked back and forth with a steady swing, although her ankles were still getting battered.

"That's it! I think you've got the idea!" encouraged Annabelle. Mandy slowly walked the length of the room and back three times, then sat down on the window ledge.

"Watch out!" cried Clarissa, but it was too late. The back of the hoop hit the wall, causing the front to fly up and hit Mandy on the forehead.

"Ouch!" she yelped, rubbing her head. "How did that happen?"

"Sitting is a whole different story. You must gather the side hoop strings in your hands and flip the hoop up in back. See, the front then stays down by your toes," instructed Clarissa, deftly flipping her hoop up as she sat on the bed.

Mandy struggled. The hoop seemed to have a mind of its own. It took a dozen tries and several more knocks on the noggin before she learned to flex her wrists, so the hoop swung up the proper distance in back.

"It will be a bit easier when you have the weight of petticoats on the hoop. I know, let's put several on now and try again," said Clarissa, tossing out some petticoats from her closet. Mandy stood, while the girls layered the garments over the hoop. She walked cautiously across the room. It was easier. The extra weight stopped the hoop from bobbing erratically, but when she sat down, the hoop caught below her bottom, and the petticoats flew up in her face.

"If that happens in the presence of a gentleman, he will have to marry you because he saw your bloomers. Maybe you better remain standing until you get the hang of it," giggled Annabelle.

Mandy had had enough. The noonday heat made the upper story stifling. The effort of working with the hoop had stimulated her body, soaking her in sweat. "That's enough for today," she said, pulling the undergarments over her head and untying the hoop strings. "If I learn everything in one day, you two won't have anything to do the rest of the summer."

"You're a good sport, Mandy," said Clarissa. "Let's ask mama if we can go wading in the creek to cool off before we are prostrate with the heat."

Wading in the creek turned out to be quite a production. Towels and a blanket to sit on had to be procured. A household servant was to accompany the girls to check for water snakes and other pests. Mandy thought of the freedom she had enjoyed on the farm. She had gone to the little pond whenever she could, all alone. Nothing bad had ever happened. All this folderol was a bit much, she decided.

The main meal was served at two o'clock. Unlike Dr. Adger's diet, the Gibbes were heavy meat eaters. Chicken, fish, pork, or lamb in one form or another was always included along with the usual vegetables and fruits. The girls did not eat sweets except on special occasions because of their tendency to gain weight.

Mandy ate sparingly. She did not want to seem to be preoccupied with food. Clarissa and Annabelle ate according to what they were wearing. If they had on their tightly laced corsets, they nibbled; if they were wearing shifts, they feasted. That was another reason not to gain weight, Mandy decided. She detested wearing a corset.

The redone lavender dress looked lovely on Mandy. The color seemed to turn her normally dark blue eyes to violet. To complete her image the girls spent hours arranging her long, brown hair. They piled it on top of her head, but that made her face look too long. Next they parted it in the middle and made banana curls on each side of her face. Somehow, that looked too fussy for her no-nonsense attitude. By general consensus they agreed that she looked best having her hair pulled to one side with several long curls hanging over her shoulder.

"Can you dance?" asked Annabelle, one evening when the girls were perched on the joggling board, enjoying the night breezes wafting across the front porch.

"No. I don't like dancing," Mandy replied. "I think it's silly, all those bends and twists. Dancing people look like wriggling worms. I'd much rather just sit and listen to the music."

"Don't be a stick-in-the-mud. Dancing is fun. You get to dress up in fancy clothes and listen to music from a trained orchestra," mused Annabelle. "I love to dance. Mama says I'm as light as a feather when I do the waltz." So saying, she hopped from the board and began twirling across the porch.

"Try to think of dancing as a method to teach your body good balance and flexibility," suggested Clarissa. "Look, see how I hold my arms while my feet move up and back? Try it, Mandy. Dancing helps make you grace-ful. It's part of our social structure, like barbecues and horse racing."

Mandy followed Clarissa's footwork. She felt a few muscles tighten in protest. It was more demanding than it looked. Step to the front, step to the side, twirl, then reverse. Soon all the girls were waltzing around the porch.

That night she woke with a start. A muscle cramp in the calf of her left leg made her hop out of bed and hobble back and forth painfully. These southern ladies look so soft, but they must be hard as nails, she thought, rubbing her leg vigorously. She was developing a new appreciation for Low Country ways.

Each week brought a new lesson. Mandy learned to curtsy and extend her gloved hand in greeting. She was amazed at the intricacies of the simple fan. Closed it meant one thing, open, another. Southern boys were taught to read the fan's signals so no social mistakes caused them embarrassment.

Learning to embroider drove Mandy frantic. She could not keep her stitches in a straight line. While the sisters spent their hour of sewing embellishing linens for their hope chests, Mandy struggled, tearing out errant stitches, as she attempted to do an alphabet sampler. She gritted her teeth as the needle stabbed her finger, or the thread tangled itself into an impossible knot. One day she flung the sampler onto a chair and walked away in a huff. Outside a steady breeze and cloudy sky promised a cooler than usual temperature. "I need to get away by myself," she said. "A walk will do me good."

Although she had seen most of Friendville by carriage, she had never walked beyond the house gardens, except the one time the girls went wading. Mrs. Gibbes said it was unseemly for a lady to go anywhere unescorted. Mandy tiptoed down the main hall and eased herself out the back door. The servants were busy in the garden and paid no notice as she walked under the grape arbor toward the wooded area. Soon, she was again breathing the spicy scent of pine, as she listened to the wind sighing gently in overhead branches. She kicked off her shoes and loosened her hair from the hairnet that kept it clean and contained. Then she began to run across the pine needle carpet, flinching when accidentally stepping on a pinecone. Finally, she came to the crest of a hill. Below was cultivated bottomland with corn, sorghum, and cotton in various stages of growth. Beyond was a wide, free-flowing stream overhung with water oaks and sycamores. Mandy plunked down on a small patch of grass and watched a turkey vulture make long, lazy spirals in the sky. It felt so good to be outside, alone. She gazed to her left to study the

Woodburn house, wondering what Dr. Adger was doing and if anyone was tending the vegetable garden as carefully as she had. She had liked living there. The work was demanding, but on her free time she had been allowed to do and go wherever she desired. At the Gibbes she felt as if she were a puppet on a string, with Mrs. Gibbes pulling her one way, and Annabelle and Clarissa, another. Was it necessary to live such a structured life?

She felt as if she was losing her individuality. She cared little about fancy embroidery, or memorizing poetry. All she did was sit—to sew, read, pray, prepare tea, and study. Her stepfather would have called it vanity and sent her to the fields. Surely there could be a happy medium. Perhaps Mrs. Gibbes would let her have a little garden of her own. Yes, that was the problem, she had nothing of her own. Almost everything except her red dress was someone's castoff. She was beginning to feel like an afterthought. She wanted to do something productive. She needed to be needed.

During supper that night, Mandy listlessly pushed her food around her plate.

"Mandy, are you well? Have you been eating green apples again?" asked Mrs. Gibbes, noticing her lack of appetite.

"No, ma'am. I'm just not hungry. May I be excused, please?"

Mrs. Gibbes nodded. Mandy carefully folded her napkin and returned her chair to its place, then went to her room. She sat on the window seat and looked out over the fields. The sunset was a fiery mixture of orange and violet with green and gold streaks radiating across the sky. She watched until the purple night clouds extinguished the brilliant display. Suddenly, there was a light knock on her door, and Mrs. Gibbes appeared.

"A penny for your thoughts," she said quietly.

Mandy continued looking out of the window. "I love living here. I'm ever so thankful you took me in," she said, her voice quivering. "I'm just not used to this way of life. I feel as if I should be working in the kitchen or garden. I think I would feel better if I were contributing something to the family."

"I see. Gardening and cooking are best left to the servants. They would feel insulted if we assigned family members or guests to their tasks. You are a family member, Mandy. I hope you realize that. I can understand your restlessness. Being productive gave you self-esteem because you are a very ambitious young woman. I have just heard of an opening for a temporary nanny, if you would be interested. Mrs. Synne, from a farm on the Three and Twenty Creek, needs help with her two children. She has redheaded twins who are quite a handful, I understand. Her husband is ill, and she is tending him day and night. It would be helpful if you looked after the girls in the afternoon to give her a rest. Perhaps you could use some of your other skills as well. They do not have any household help."

"I don't know much about children, but I reckon I can learn," said Mandy.

"That's settled, then. I'll send Jacob with a note to tell Mrs. Synne you will be arriving tomorrow after dinner and will stay until seven o'clock. That should lighten her load."

Chapter Ten

"Mama! Mama! A strange lady is here!" shouted a red haired youngster, wearing a muddy pinafore. Another girl the same age, size, and looks peered around a porch railing and watched silently as Mandy climbed out of the buggy and approached the farm house. She gently knocked on the door and waited, looking around to pass the time and quiet her nerves. How different this farm was from the Gibbes. There was nothing growing here just for show. The front yard was a mix of ragged grass and weeds. A few untrimmed shrubs graced the walkway, and the usual oaks offered cooling shade. The one-story clapboard house was spartan in appearance with a high center roof to encourage the summer heat to rise above its occupants. The porch went across the front of the house only, shading two tall narrow windows on each side of the front door.

A slight rustling caused Mandy to turn around. A plain, slim woman with faded red hair stood in the doorway. Her face was etched with lines of weariness and stress.

"Mrs. Synne? I'm Mandy. I've come to tend your girls for a while."

"Won't you come in, Mandy. I can't tell you how grateful I am to you for coming. I've got my hands full nursing my husband, and the girls are running wild. My

husband cut his leg with a scythe. It has become infected.
The doctor had to cut out a small piece of flesh, and I
must clean the wound and dress it several times a day,
besides trying to keep the farm going. I'm plumb tuckered
out!"

Mandy recognized the strained look in Mrs. Synne's
eyes and the stoop to her shoulders. Her ma had looked
the same—symptoms of being overworked and undernour-
ished. She smiled brightly.

"I'm sure the girls and I will get along just fine. Don't
you worry; I'll take them for a little walk, and then we'll
play on the swing."

"Could you bathe them before you leave tonight? I'll
put out their nightgowns. If they are hungry, there is
bread and preserves on the kitchen table. Oh, their names
are Sally and Susie."

Mandy nodded and returned to the front porch where
the twins sat playing "Cats-in-the-Cradle" with a piece of
string.

"That's very good," said Mandy as she sat beside them
watching the string take different shapes between their
nimble fingers. Suddenly the game ended and the girls
tugged at Mandy's arms.

"Come see Cleo, our pig. She just had babies," urged
Susie. Mandy allowed herself to be pulled toward the
pigpen in the side yard. A large black and white sow lay
on her side, while ten little piglets satisfied their hunger
with loud sucking noises and high pitched squeals.

"Mama said not to name the babies 'cause she will sell
most of them," said Sally, softly. "I hope she doesn't sell
the one with the black floppy ear. That's my favorite."

"I like the one with the extra curl in its tail. I've
already named her Curly-Shirley," boasted Susie. "That's
my pig, and nobody gets her but me! Tell us a story, Miss
Mandy. A story, please."

The afternoon sped by as Mandy dealt with the she-nanigans of the 4-year-old twins. By the time they had been bathed and fed, she was exhausted. She could have cheered when she saw Jacob arrive with the buggy to take her home.

The change in her attitude was remarkable now that she had something challenging to do. The first week at the Synne's she spent getting to know the family. They were from central Pennsylvania, where they had attempted to homestead forty acres of rocky, infertile soil. They were too poor to hire help, so they existed on whatever they could grow. One day, Mr. Synne met a surveyor who had just recently returned from the South. His description of fertile land and gracious living fired Mr. Synne's imagination, and off they went looking for the Garden of Eden. They found the land to be everything the surveyor said it was, but it still had to be worked diligently before it would yield its bounty. The Synne's did not believe in owning slaves, and they could not afford to hire help so they were in much the same situation as they had been in Pennsylvania. "Except the weather is better," stated Mrs. Synne.

Susie and Sally were fraternal twins, each having somewhat distinct features and individual personalities.

"I was born first," bragged Susie. "I'm the oldest by ten minutes. I'm the boss." She was very aggressive and quite the tomboy. Mandy learned to look for Susie in the trees surrounding the house or out by the livestock pens where she was constantly trying to ride anything that moved. Her clothes were usually stained, her hands and face streaked with dirt, but she had a quick mind and was up to any challenge.

Sally was the reticent one, the daydreamer. She gladly let Susie be the leader. Mandy often found her on the swing pensively sucking her thumb. Sally was quiet, but she stuck to a task until she completed it.

Mandy was intuitive enough to realize that the success of the girls in the local school and in Pendleton society depended on their awareness of local customs just as it did for her. She tried to make a game of the manners they were required to know. The girls loved playing dress-up with some of Annabelle's and Clarissa's castoffs and eagerly learned their social obligations as part of the make-believe.

One day, Mandy brought them some winter squash. "Let's make something fancy for supper," she suggested. She showed the girls how to peel the squash and cook it. Then she mashed it, adding honey and grated apple.

"Yum!" said Susie, taking a big spoonful. "This tastes good all the way down! Can we keep the seeds and plant them?"

"We'll have to dry them first." Mandy rinsed the seeds with water, removing the pulp, then put them on a piece of paper, and set them in the pie cupboard. Sally busied herself scooping a large helping of the squash into a bowl.

"Papa will like this," she said. "Maybe it will help him get better." She carefully carried the bowl to his bedroom. A few minutes later, Mrs. Synne appeared with the empty bowl.

"Miss Mandy, that concoction was delicious! Please feel free to use the kitchen whenever you want. I'm afraid I cook a rather plain meal. I'm sure we all will appreciate a little variety."

Mandy blushed at the praise. She did like to cook and had invented many unusual dishes to keep food palatable for her stepfather. She could make some of those recipes to help this family eat better.

That week she and the twins went foraging. "Look for anything that might be edible," she told the twins. They picked late apples, pears, wild grapes, and nuts. She showed them how to mix several different fruits together in a sugar syrup then put biscuits on top and bake them. The Synnes had plenty of eggs from their chickens, so Mandy made custards and meringues, not to mention her favorite—sugar cake. She was in her glory. The twins stood watching or helped stir. By the time the recipe was finished, all three of them wore traces of the ingredients on their faces.

Weeks went by. Mandy set herself a rigid schedule, so she would not neglect her lessons at the Gibbes. She studied basic French, read the classics, practiced the piano, and continued sewing. Mrs. Gibbes showed her how to make her own nightgowns and underwear. She enjoyed making something practical.

Her circle of acquaintances grew as she attended the various church functions. She was still the brunt of Annabelle's jokes and Clarissa's corrections, but all of life was enhanced by the time she spent in the Synne household. They were people she understood. There, she was needed and appreciated.

It was mid-October before Mr. Synne could walk. He had an obvious limp, but most of the muscle had been saved, so he was able to return to farming. For a while, Mandy helped in the kitchen, drying fruit and making preserves. She tried to make herself indispensable as she did not want to leave her second family, as she called them.

Susie and Sally celebrated their birthday November 1. Mandy brought a beef roast from the Gibbes. She made dried fruit compote, spoon-bread, and a decorated sugar cake overflowing with red and white icing. The girls were delighted. Annabelle and Clarissa had contributed several primary readers, so the girls could learn their letters. Mr. Synne had made them whistles and fancy wooden hair combs with their names carved on them. Carving had given him something to do while he was bedridden. He had a box full of beautiful carved objects, including a pecan wood chess set which he hoped to sell at a handsome price.

After the dinner was over and the girls had said their thank yous, they went to check on some newly hatched chicks. Mr. Synne handed a package wrapped in brown paper to Mandy saying, "You've been such a help to the missus and twins. This is a little something to show our appreciation."

Mandy was speechless. She tore the paper off and gasped with delight. It was a memory box—a place to keep objects from special occasions. The top of the walnut box had been carved in birds and flowers. She opened the lid and discovered two locks of hair tied with different colored ribbons.

"That's from Susie and Sally, so you won't forget them," said Mrs. Synne softly, tears gathering in her eyes. "I don't know how I would have managed if you hadn't come. Truly, I was at my wit's end."

Mandy realized the party had been a double celebration—the twins' fifth birthday and her termination as a nanny. She sat quietly, staring at the box and waiting for the lump in her throat to disappear. "This is the nicest gift I have ever gotten," she said. "I loved every minute of being here. I hope you will remember me if you ever need help again. Sally and Susie have become like little sisters. I will miss you all very much. Perhaps you won't mind if I come for a visit once in a while." Mandy lovingly stroked the box. Here was something that had been made especially for her. A reward, payment, really, for services rendered. She had proven her worth to the Synnes.

"Miss Mandy! Jacob's coming!" shouted Susie from the front porch.

Holding the box tightly against her chest, Mandy walked to the porch. "Good-bye, girls. Enjoy your books.

Your ma said you will be starting school soon. Study hard. Be good little helpers to your ma. I'll come see you when I can."

"We will. Bye, Miss Mandy, we'll miss you," they chorused, waving vigorously as Jacob set the horse to trotting. Mandy waved until they were out of sight then settled against the seat with a sigh. What would she do now to prove her worth?

Chapter Eleven

It was Christmas week. The pie pantry was overflowing with fruitcakes, cream tarts, dried apple pies, and an assortment of cookies. Mandy, Annabelle, and Clarissa, under Mrs. Gibbes supervision, had decorated every possible inch of their house. Magnolia leaves and holly branches with shiny red berries covered the mantles; dried corn leaves twisted into the shapes of flowers and bows nestled in pine branches; fancy wreaths of natural greenery, straw flowers, and nuts decorated the doors. Marzipan topiaries sat on tables laden with fine china and shining silver. Guests and relatives had been dropping in to pay holiday greetings off and on for days.

Tonight, the girls were going to their first adult Christmas ball at the opera house, the upper floor of the large general store just across the street. There would be an orchestra, a midnight buffet, and dancing. For days they had been discussing what finery to wear. Now pandemonium reigned as Annabelle and Clarissa rushed from one room to the other, issuing orders to Ruby, their household maid, as she tied, buttoned, and coifed. Necklaces, fans, hairbows, gloves, and hankies lay on the bed. Perfume, powder, and sachets sat on the dressing table. Did the pearl necklace look good with green? Perhaps a gold pendant would be better.... Mandy stood to one side watching the sisters' toilette with amusement. What did it matter whether they wore gold or silver or if the earbobs were long and dangling or button clips? She was glad of her simple wardrobe. Mrs. Gibbes had given her a midnight blue velvet dress, remade, of course. It had a sweetheart neckline embellished with silver embroidery in the shape of ivy leaves. Silver buttons cascaded down the front, ending six inches above the hem where the dress was caught up by a bow, revealing an insert of fine silver lace. The design was simple elegance. She wore her hair pulled to one side, its long ringlets held with a silver ribbon. Around her neck she wore her mother's cross now hanging from a silver chain discarded by Clarissa because she thought it too coarse. It suited Mandy just fine. She pulled on cream-colored pigskin gloves, selected a white lace fan with silver gilt edges, and a hankie with blue tatting then pronounced herself ready.

One by one, the girls descended the stairs. Mr. and Mrs. Gibbes awaited them with words of admiration and encouragement.

"Ladies, you will be the belles of the ball," predicted Mr. Gibbes, as he escorted them to the covered phaeton.

"Just be yourselves on your best behavior. Dance with every gentleman who asks you, do not play favorites," admonished Mrs. Gibbes as they rode along.

Mandy shuddered at the mention of dancing. She had practiced the quadrille and the waltz, but the idea of close contact with the opposite sex made her nauseous.

After a short ride, the general store came into view. From every window the soft glow of candles radiated a heartfelt welcome. Like the Gibbes' house, the opera area was decorated with natural greenery. Crystal chandeliers refracted the brightness of the fireplace flames, casting festive light patterns upon the high ceilings. Fruits glazed with egg white and sugar glistened on a sideboard where a huge punch bowl surrounded by candies, cookies, and tiny petit fours offered refreshment. The large oriental rugs and plush chairs had been removed, revealing freshly waxed, heart-pine floors.

The ladies in their colorful hoop dresses and the gentlemen with their brocade vests and velvet jackets made a kaleidoscope of color. Everyone was sharing holiday greetings, making the commotion almost too much for Mandy. When the necessary introductions had been made, Annabelle and Clarissa left to join their friends. Mandy moved to a far corner of the room, distancing herself from all the activity. Here, she could study the people without seeming to stare. She knew most of them; the Low Country community of Pendleton was not that large, and many of them attended the same church. Still, being dressed in their finest made the people seem somehow more imposing.

"I see I'm not the only people watcher here tonight," said a deep, male voice behind her. Mandy gave a start.

"Oh, Dr. Stuart, you surprised me. It's just so lovely; I can't take it all in. I'm not used to such pomp and circumstance."

"Don't be intimidated by all the curtsying and bowing. Tonight we are playing dress-up; mostly for the ladies' benefit, of course. They deserve mollycoddling once in a while. We gents would much rather meet over a good card game, some expensive whiskey, and imported cigars."

Mandy smiled. Her thoughts wandered to the Synnes. How were they celebrating Christmas? Had Mrs. Synne found time to make the twins the new dresses she had promised them?

"Cousin Jim, aren't you going to introduce me to this lovely young lady?" asked a sandy haired young man in a forest green jacket and tan pants, who stood at least a head taller than Mandy.

"By all means, Smith. Miss Mandy Greene, may I present Mr. Smith LaFarge from Beaufort. Mr. LaFarge is here looking for a parcel of land to purchase for the cultivation of cotton, a most profitable endeavor, especially since we have the Pendleton cloth mill in operation. Mr. Smith LaFarge, please meet Miss Mandy Greene." To simplify things, Mandy had agreed to go by her mother's maiden name while staying in Pendleton. Mandy offered her gloved hand as she had practiced many times. Smith bowed and lightly grasped her hand. Mandy felt like fleeing out the back door, but instead curtsied gracefully.

"How long have you been staying in Pendleton?" asked Smith. "Could you acquaint me with some families interested in selling property? I know you ladies often have inside information."

Mandy ignored the first question and avoided any direct answer to the second. "Pendleton is such a lovely town. Progressive, too. There is talk the railroad will be coming through soon. The land is fertile and productive, so I'm sure your plans to grow cotton will be successful. Have you found the area to your liking?"

"Yes, I'm enjoying my stay. The hotel is more than satisfactory. The air is very clean and dry here, and I've never seen so many varieties of birds. Are you a bird watcher, Miss Greene?"

"I enjoy being out-of-doors. The fields of Friendville make for pleasant walking. On a clear day the distant mountains are beautiful."

"You must show me the view one day, when I have finished my quest for tillable land. The orchestra has begun playing. May I have this waltz?"

"I'm afraid I am unable to dance tonight due to an injury to my foot. Clarissa or Annabelle would be more than happy to take my place. They are over by the settee in the green and gold dresses. Please excuse me."

Mandy's face was red with shame for lying, but she just could not bring herself to dance with any man. She curtsied then turned, walking quickly, but with a little limp to validate her condition. Once away from the festivities she relaxed and wandered into an adjoining room. Here, on a cozy chintz sofa, she listened to the music and tried to picture herself mingling with the guests. She decided she was too immature to participate in such grown-up celebrations. The dress made her look older and sophisticated, but inside she was still a young girl. She closed her eyes, letting the music waft over her.

"Mandy! We've been looking all over for you! Imagine finding you sitting alone. What's the matter? Are you ill? Perhaps your corset is laced too tightly. The midnight buffet is being served. Nana Stuart made many of the special dishes. If you think her Sunday dinners are delicious, wait 'til you taste her party fare. Mama says you must learn to circulate and converse intelligently with strangers; not that there are many strangers here." Annabelle paused for breath, then grabbed Mandy's arm and drew her toward the doorway.

"Stop pulling! You'll tear my sleeve. I'll come have some supper; I just don't feel like dancing."

"Well, at least bring a plate and socialize with the girls from church. Otherwise, your rude behavior will be the talk of the town and a poor reflection on Mama."

Mandy certainly did not want to embarrass Mrs. Gibbes so, filling a plate, she joined the other girls and pretended she was having a good time. She tried giggling at a funny comment, while nervously flicking her fan, but the harder she attempted to blend in the more miserable she felt. When the music started again, she walked with an exaggerated limp to where the older women were sitting. Turning her back slightly to the dancers, she pretended to be very interested in one lady's tatting.

The Southern men, having been trained by their mothers to read between the lines, silently accepted Mandy's wish to be left alone and ignored her. When Mrs. Gibbes finally indicated it was time to depart, Mandy was the first to get her shawl and thank Dr. and Mrs. Stuart for sponsoring such a lovely evening.

"I daresay you've enjoyed other evenings more," observed Nana Stuart. "Perhaps next year you will feel more comfortable in mixed company. Annabelle and Clarissa, along with the other young ladies, have been socializing with the opposite sex since they started taking dancing lessons years ago. Southern boys of class are taught to be gentlemen. You need not fear."

Mandy smiled weakly. Her past experiences with her stepfather were proving to be a stumbling block to her present social responsibilities. Somehow she had to break free from his influence on her subconscious.

Christmas Eve found almost everyone in Pendleton in the church. Mandy listened as the pastor read the Christmas story from the Gospel of Luke. The birth of the Christ Child had been so unassuming. His life one of total dependence upon His Heavenly Father. How could the Gibbes, serious Christians that they were, encourage their daughters to place such an emphasis on their looks, clothes, and expensive possessions? What did the Low Country customs have to do with God's command to love Him above all else? True, the Gibbes did give to the needy in the community, but in her opinion, they loved themselves first, God, second. She thought of Soaring Hawk dressed in deerskins, sitting on the rock thanking the Great Spirit for the goodness of the day. The simplicity of his worship somehow seemed more fitting than the fancy clothes and intricate rituals of which she had become a part. Would she ever be able to make sense of it all?

When the last carol had been sung and the congregation was departing amid wishes for a Merry Christmas,
Mandy noticed Smith LaFarge talking earnestly with Dr.
Stuart. She averted her eyes in the chance he should recognize her. He had not claimed his walk in the fields, and
she did not want to encourage him. At twenty-one, he
was far too old and sophisticated for the likes of her. Yet
she had to admit his fair, curly hair, fashionable side-
burns, broad shoulders, and neat appearance were appealing.

After a delicious Christmas brunch that Mandy could
not fully enjoy because of the corset that nipped her waist
into a tiny seventeen inches, the Gibbes gathered in the
library to open their gifts. Mandy had persuaded Mr.
Synne to build and carve a cigar humidor that she gave to
Dr. Gibbes who was greatly impressed with the intricate
details of the carved hunt scene on its lid. She presented
Mrs. Gibbes with several jars of wild berry jelly including
elderberry that the Gibbes had never tasted. Annabelle
and Clarissa were the recipients of honey suckle and rose
sachets on which she had embroidered their names. In
return she received earrings, material for some under-
clothes, and new shoes which she desperately needed. From
the Stuarts, she was given a small book of Psalms and kid
gloves. She sensed the family was respecting her desire to
live simplistically. After all, she was merely an orphan
receiving food and fellowship from a kind family.

There was another church service to attend in the
afternoon, then a light supper with some of the Gibbes'
friends. Annabelle and Clarissa joined the other church
youth at a boxing party where clothes, candy, and other
goodies were boxed up to give to the plantation slaves and
house servants. Boxing Day, as it was called, was the day
after Christmas. It was an old English custom that had
come to America with the early settlers and seemed espe-

cially suited to the South. Mandy had never heard of the tradition, but thought it was a good one. The slaves enjoyed very few of life's amenities. Except for a small garden plot per family, they were totally dependent on their masters for the necessities of life.

The next morning, all the slaves of Friendville gathered first at the Stuarts, then at the Gibbes for their gifts. The children squealed with delight as they were given marzipan and taffy wrapped in colorful paper. It was a day to rest and enjoy family and friends.

The weather gifted them with sunny skies and warm temperatures, so Mandy escaped to the fields for some quiet time. To her great surprise she encountered Smith at the crest of the hill staring down at the creek and bottomland.

"Miss Greene, how nice! It seems we will enjoy a walk together after all. Or would you prefer your own company?"

"I'd be delighted to have your companionship," Mandy said politely, although she would have preferred to walk alone.

"What do you think of Friendville? Is it a thriving plantation? Are the slaves industrious and obedient?"

"I really can't answer those questions. Dr. Stuart is the one to ask. I have been in Pendleton just a little more than a year. However, I have not heard of any disturbances."

"Good. I think father will be very pleased with my recommendation to purchase Mountain View plantation. In my opinion, it is one of the best plantations in the area. Its fields seem well suited for the growing of cotton. Pendleton is a lovely town. The Low Country element adds the necessary charm and culture to make living here an enjoyable experience."

Mandy nodded absently. "When will you know for sure if the sale will go through?"

"By spring, I imagine. I have money to put down on the property as a binder to hold it until father sees it for himself. If he is pleased, work will begin right away. I will live here in the summer and in Beaufort in the winter. May I call on you after I've settled my affairs?"

"I don't know. I'm only fifteen," Mandy stammered, blushing. "I don't think I'm ready for male friendship yet. Perhaps Clarissa might be more suitable. . . ." With tears of frustration welling up, she gathered up her skirts and began to run, not stopping until she reached the back gardens of the Gibbes' house. Yet, try as she might, she had not been able to run away from her fears. They followed her into the house like puppies nipping at her heels.

Chapter Twelve

The winter days passed quickly. Mandy crammed as much learning as possible into every minute. On days when Mrs. Gibbes went visiting and the girls were being tutored, she cajoled the cook into teaching her the finer points of southern cuisine. She practiced coddling eggs, made a coconut cake, and roasted a suckling pig. She turned plain biscuits into a dessert for peaches by adding brown sugar, cinnamon, and pecans to the mixture. She spent hours studying. What she couldn't understand she memorized.

Three afternoons a week she tutored Susie and Sally, in order to pay back the Synnes for the presents they had made for her to give to the Gibbes at Christmas. She found great satisfaction in helping the twins with their studies. She tried to be creative, to make the lessons interesting and relevant. The girls quickly progressed under her instruction.

The winter weather was as fickle as Clarissa was about her new beau. One day it was warm and sunny, the next day it rained, then came sleet or snow, only to be forgotten as the sun warmed the earth once again. Mandy loved the garden's winter display. There was something blooming all the time—susanquas, camellias, forsythia, witch hazel, daphnes, and bulbs of all sorts. Mrs. Gibbes kept fresh flowers in every formal room of the house.

"Mandy, do sit down for a minute. I declare you are in a total frenzy these days. You must rest your mind or you will have a nervous breakdown," admonished Mrs. Gibbes one morning as she watched Mandy walk back and forth trying to conjugate French verbs. Mandy smiled and sat on the needlepoint cushion indicated by her mistress.

"I'm trying to catch up with my studies, so I'll be in Annabelle's class next year. It's embarrassing to be so old and know so little."

"My dear, you know more than both those silly girls put together because you understand human nature. Your past life has made you wise beyond your years. There is a look of maturity in your face that is usually not found in women until they are in their late twenties. I'm sure that is why Smith was attracted to you. You needn't blush. He truly did not suspect how young you are. Fifteen is much too early to have a serious beau. Look at Clarissa at seventeen; she is making life miserable for all of us with her on-again, off-again relationship with Harrison. There are days I'm tempted to ship her off to a convent." Mandy laughed at the mental image of Clarissa in a wimple.

"Seriously, Mandy, I have noticed a change in you. You seem so driven. Of what are you afraid? You used to occasionally socialize with the church young people. Now you hardly ever leave the house except to visit the Synnes. Are you unhappy in Pendleton? Do you want to leave us?"

"Oh no, ma'am! Being with you is almost like being with family. But I realize I can't enjoy your favors forever. I must be prepared to go it alone one day."

"Poor child! We will make a special effort this coming summer to search for your relatives. Surely, with all the people who migrate here from Charleston, someone must remember some living relatives of Cornelia Drake and her family. Don't fret. God is looking out for you, of that I'm sure." Smiling gently, Mrs. Gibbes pressed Mandy's hand in hers for a moment, then left the room.

"God is looking out for you," echoed in Mandy's mind. "God, if you really care about me, please help me find my kin. I want to belong to someone, really belong," she whispered into the air. She paused, half expecting a reply or a sign from heaven, but she heard nothing except the sound of her own breathing.

February arrived and with it came plans for a Valentine party to be held at the Cherry Hotel for all the young people of Pendleton. Mandy expressed surprise that Annabelle and Clarissa were not more excited about the occasion.

"We have to dress down," explained Annabelle, in an aristocratic tone of voice. "Mama won't let us wear anything that would suggest ostentisity. We will wear some of our nicer everyday clothes. How boring! Everyone knows the Low Country society is wealthy. But proper etiquette dictates we keep our materialism to ourselves. Bah!"

"The party really is great fun, Mandy," said Clarissa. "You must go with us. Everyone will be there. No one puts on airs except this silly goose." She threw a pillow at her sister. "The mountain music is lively, and there will be a barbecue."

"I hope Elise is there again this year. She is the best clogger in the whole state of South Carolina. Her feet move so quickly that you can hardly see them. I must admit I enjoy the music. It's so happy." Annabelle hopped up humming a tune, keeping time with her feet. Grabbing Mandy by the hands the two of them swung in circles until, breathless, they collapsed on the bed.

"I'll go if I don't have to wear a corset," said Mandy. "I feel as if I'm in a torture chamber when I'm laced into those stays."

"No corset or hoop necessary," laughed Clarissa. "But you are so tall and thin, someone might mistake you for a boy if you don't wear something feminine. With your dark hair a red dress would be very flattering. Let's see what I can find." Clarissa invaded her closet, tossing out anything of a red color. Mandy waited silently. She was tired of hand-me-downs. She wanted a new dress of her own.

As if reading her mind, Clarissa poked at the pile of clothes. "None of these will suit. Let's ask mama if we can pick out some material and make you a dress. You can chose the fabric and style."

In the end, Mandy decided on a royal blue cotton sateen with pale blue lace trim. She chose a simple princess style but added two rows of ruffles along the curved bodice yoke to enhance her bosom. The sleeves puffed at the top, then became formfitting below the elbow. The hem included an eight-inch ruffle that just skirted her ankles. The blue color electrified her dark blue eyes and emphasized her rosy complexion. Mandy put it on, and declared she truly felt like a queen bee.

The party was all Clarissa said it to be. Almost every young person in the Pendleton area attended. The ballroom was filled to capacity; the overflow gathered on the porch. The air was filled with the music of violins, dulcimers, guitars, and flutes. Mandy watched the musicians for a while, then wandered outside where many of the young people were clustered according to topic of discussion or acquaintance. Smiling, she moved among the girls, listening to their gossip, then stood near enough to a boys' gathering to hear them excitedly debate the issue of industrializing the South.

"I say the elite ought to have the last word," argued a redheaded lad. "Our whole way of living will be changed forever if we adopt the new inventions and business practices of the North. If we had to pay our people wages, we surely could not afford the lifestyle we enjoy now. Besides, our slaves are our property, not hired hands."

"Then we will be like Europe, a loose conglomerate of individual states, each with their own laws. We need a strong central monetary system for financial stability. Our thinking should be what is progress for one is progress for all," stated another.

As the discussion became more intense, Mandy walked away for fear the challenge of a duel might be forthcoming. She could not understand why differences had to be settled violently. The Low Country customs had been adopted from the French Huguenots, who had settled the coastal areas after being hunted and slaughtered throughout Europe. If anything, the Low Country men should be pacifists, she thought, but instead they often chose dueling to emphasize their opinions. By and large they were very protective of women, and materialism added no weight to a man's acceptance in society. Rich or poor, a man acting under their code of a gentleman was accepted by Pendleton society. The unrefined were ignored. She had to admit, the town flourished under these traditions.

"Mandy! There you are! Come watch Elise clog. She is going to do a special selection with bag pipe accompaniment," called Annabelle, leaning over the porch railing. Mandy entered the hotel lobby. People were lining the walls three and four deep watching a young girl in a plaid kilt tap her feet and twirl to the howling music of the pipes. The faster the rhythm, the faster her feet moved, until her whole body was consumed by the beat. Braids flapping, skirt swirling, she looked like a miniature whirlwind. Suddenly, the music stopped, leaving Elise gasping for breath. Everyone clapped wildly then began pairing up for a Virginia reel. Clarissa pushed Mandy into the girls' line.

"Just do what everyone else does," she said, grabbing Mandy's right hand while someone else held her left hand. One by one the girls and boys in sets danced their way through several patterns. Ignoring her partner, Mandy concentrated on the dance and made no mistakes. It was easy, after watching several others do the steps first. For the first time she began to enjoy herself. By the end of the evening she was relaxed and smiling. Several girls her age had conversed with her and promised to visit in the near future. Now that she knew what was expected of her, she no longer felt so threatened.

The month of March brought an unsettling surprise. One evening after supper Dr. Gibbes asked everyone to remain at the table.

"As you know, Dr. and Nana Stuart are getting on in years and Nana has not felt her best recently. She has a heartfelt desire to return to Beaufort, the town of her birth. We do not think it wise for them to make the journey alone or to be that far away from their only child, so we have decided to move to the Beaufort area also. There are many opportunities for me as a doctor, and land is still available for farming. You girls will have many more opportunities, than are found here. The move will benefit everyone.

"I will be leaving shortly to secure property and prepare for the building of a new house," continued Dr. Gibbes. "Your mother has agreed to oversee the packing and moving preparations for us and Nana Stuart. I trust you young ladies will be as helpful as possible. I will return in July with a progress report. This is a great opportunity for all of you; yes, Mandy, you are included. The Low Country schools are far superior to those in this area. I am sure you will come to agree with me, after you have experienced the amenities awaiting you."

As soon as they were dismissed, Clarissa and Annabelle went to their rooms chattering excitedly. Mandy slipped out the front door and stood on the porch, trying to sort out her feelings. On the one hand, she would have to start over again to find acceptance among strangers. But on a happier note, she would be nearer to the location where her relatives lived. Perhaps she was nearing the end of her quest. She decided to approach the whole situation positively. At least she was included in the moving plans, so they were not abandoning her. She took a deep breath of the pine scented air. Life was what one made of it; she would make hers successful.

Her acceptance into Pendleton society came none too soon. Dr. and Mrs. Gibbes spent their free time working on the plans for their new house, leaving the girls to their own devices. The days passed by pleasantly for Mandy, as she visited with the young women of Pendleton and took tea on many a piazza in town. By the end of the month, Dr. Gibbes was ready to make the two hundred mile trek in search of land suitable for his family. His father-in-law had inherited a small plantation, so there was no need to worry about his accommodations. With several servants, a buggy, and a pair of matched gray horses, he set forth one fine morning while the family shouted encouragement and waved good-by from the porch. As they re-entered the house, Mrs. Gibbes corralled the girls.

"We must have a meeting to discuss our plans for packing. I know we won't be leaving until October, but I don't want to wait until the last moment to make all the final decisions. We can at least weed out those items we do not wish to take with us. Clarissa and Annabelle, please go through your clothes and bring me everything that is too small or otherwise unsuitable to wear. I will have them washed and repaired. The best clothes we will send to missions. The rest we can pass out among the help.

"Mandy, you have little enough as it is. I think we had better use some of your earnings from your employment at Woodburn to prepare a proper wardrobe for you. Beaufort society is not quite as forgiving as Pendleton's residents. Should you find your family, you will be presented at a party or ball. Then there are the courtesy calls and the many church functions. You need to be prepared."

Mandy was reluctant to part with a single hard-earned penny. She had several everyday dresses plus her red wool, royal blue sateen, and midnight blue velvet for good. Her undergarments were serviceable, and she had shoes for everyday, a black leather pair for good and some lovely slippers Nana Stuart had given her. She was better dressed than she had ever been and was completely satisfied.

Nevertheless, Mrs. Gibbes insisted on adding two more day dresses and one special occasion dress. "Things are less expensive here," she said, understanding Mandy's need for financial security.

By June, Mandy finished tutoring the Synne twins and turned her attention to rounding out her own education. She had not found history very interesting until she began reading from Dr. Gibbes' library. Europe in the Middle Ages fascinated her. Particularly appealing was the plight of the French Huguenots, during the reign of the French king, Louis XIV. With tongue in cheek, he promised these educated Protestants freedom of religion, then when they began to worship openly, he captured them and had them beheaded. Panic stricken, some hid high above a river in caves, which were accessible only by rope ladders. Here they were protected and fed by sympathetic local farmers who kept their location a secret. Many who finally escaped came to America and settled mainly along the southern coast and Canada. France lost one whole generation of scientists and educators by persecuting this sect.

Summer meant a release from studying for Clarissa and Annabelle, who crammed as much socializing as possible into the remaining time before their departure. But Mandy, determined to continue her education in the grade level suitable to her age, constantly read.

True to his word, Dr. Gibbes returned in July to report that all was nicely progressing. He had found several hundred acres suitable for growing rice in Prince William Parish, a few miles from Beaufort. It was a favorite area for the elite, and large houses of exquisite beauty dotted the countryside. He had engaged an English builder who was gifted in woodworking and design. The house was scheduled for completion in mid-September. While he was in Pendleton, he sold Friendville to Dr. Adger's brother who purchased the house for his widowed sister-in-law, while at the same time incorporating some of the land into the Woodburn property.

By September, the serious packing had begun. Since the Stuarts were traveling with them, the trip became something of caravan size. Almost all the household help was accompanying them along with some of the slaves who were skilled in wrought iron and carpentry. The rest of the field hands went to Woodburn, because rice cultivation on the Low Country rivers required skills they did not have.

Nana Stuart was thrilled at the prospect of 'going home' as she called it. Wagon after wagon was filled with her fine furniture and china. As she was constantly asking advice of her adopted daughter, Mandy found herself acting as courier, traveling between houses several times a day.

The last week of September Dr. Gibbes returned, bringing with him the exciting news of the new house completed and awaiting its eager occupants. Mandy listened as he described the spacious rooms with high ceilings and large windows, the flying staircase, fireplaces with Italian marble hearths, cypress wood floors covered by oriental rugs, and indoor wash rooms. It sounded too good to be true. He also had taken the time to have his father-in-law's house cleaned and repaired. It, too, was in move-in condition.

By the second week of October, everyone was ready to travel. Six wagons manned by servants, a phaeton, and two surreys pulled by the best of their horseflesh left Pendleton amid the best wishes of friends and neighbors who for weeks had been calling, regaling them with gifts of food and personal items as remembrances.

"I've never known Pendleton to be in any state of conflict," remarked Dr. Gibbes as he waved good-by to wellwishers lining the streets. "Even in Beaufort, Pendleton is known as a city of peace and prosperity. I shall miss this beautiful place."

Mandy sat with Clarissa, Annabelle, and Ruby in one of the surreys. Her heart beat faster in anticipation of renewing the search for her relatives. She glanced at Clarissa, who was having a hard time leaving her beau, Harrison. She kept wiping away errant tears that threatened to trickle down her face.

"Clarissa, for heaven's sake, cheer up," admonished Annabelle. "Harrison said he would do his best to come for Christmas. That's only two months away. Perhaps he will attend a college in Charleston next year. In the meantime, absence makes the heart grow fonder, they say."

"Hush up!" rebuked Clarissa in a watery voice. "If you were serious about any young man here, you would be weeping and wailing at the top of your lungs. Probably tearing out your hair, too."

Mandy smiled at the truth of Clarissa's words. Annabelle thrived on theatrics. Everything that happened to her always had ten times the impact it would have on anyone else. It would take a strong man to put up with Annabelle's histrionics.

It took eleven days to make the journey to Beaufort. Although they could have taken a train from Columbia to

Charleston, Nana Stuart insisted on traveling the whole way by buggy as this was her last journey, and she wanted to see old friends along the way. Each night the Gibbes and Stuarts stayed in a hotel or with friends or relatives. The servants pitched tents or slept in the barns. Clarissa and Annabelle thrived on the excitement of encounters with various people. Mandy stayed in the background, trying to be as helpful as possible without attracting attention to herself. She was tired of retelling her life story; it made her feel like an outsider. She had kept several of Dr. Gibbes' books with her personal belongings so each night as soon as it was permissible after supper, she went to her room and read.

Every day seemed to bring a change in the terrain. By the time they reached Columbia, the land had become rather flat with great pine forests and sandy soil. Five days outside Beaufort, Mandy discovered Spanish moss. The gray, curly strands hanging from the tree branches gave the woods an ethereal quality. As soon as she could, she picked up a piece that had fallen to the ground.

"Best not put that near your belongings," called Mrs. Gibbes. "There are usually tiny spiders and other pesky varmints living in the strands."

Mandy examined it closely. Sure enough, two tiny red spiders emerged from the moss as she separated the strands so she threw the clump away in disgust. It was better to admire it from afar.

The weather had cooperated with their journey. The days were sunny and warm, the nights cool and clear. It rained only once and that was in the wee hours of the morning. The road they took was a busy one, being part of the original Cherokee trail that ran from Keowee, near Pendleton, to Port Royal on the coast. Other families and businessmen came and went. Each traveler was greeted courteously with inquiries about their health and destination. Several times Mrs. Gibbes passed out food to those who found themselves in short supply. Mandy felt proud to be part of such a loving, giving family.

Just outside Charleston the road divided. They took the right fork that bypassed the bustling seaport. Mandy could hardly disguise her disappointment.

"Don't worry. We will be coming to Charleston once we are settled. Mama will need household items that won't be found in Beaufort," whispered Clarissa, noting the look on Mandy's face.

Here, the air smelled different. The piney smell was replaced by the sharper, pungent scent of the muddy salt flats. Mandy stared at the saltwater marshes with the open canals wandering through the reedy areas. How flat the land was! The soil was light grey, powdery sand. When the wind blew sharply small eddies of fine silt rose from the plowed fields creating miniature dust devils. Live oaks, like silent sentinels, thrust their huge moss draped branches over the road, bringing welcome shade from the still piercing rays of the October sun. It was a scene that both captivated and repelled Mandy. The dense tropical undergrowth and swamps spelled disaster for anyone unfamiliar with its characteristics. Her days of walking carefree through the woods would be curtailed if the plantation property were like this, she thought.

"Here we are," shouted Dr. Gibbes to the girls in the buggy behind him. A wide, ornate wooden gate supported by tabby pillars barred the entrance to a sandy carriage path. As the gate opened, Mandy saw nothing but pines, oaks, and scrub lining the road. After a quarter of a mile, a sharp left turn caused the girls to crane their necks in anticipation.

"There's the house! I see it! Oh, isn't it beautiful!" exclaimed Annabelle, standing to get a better view. A large two-story house with huge pillars supporting a wrap-

around porch came into view. It sat on a small hill and
was surrounded by newly planted shrubs and trees. A large,
winding stairway graced the front of the house, while
double windows with carved headers on each story added
to its imposing atmosphere. The front double doors were
made of cypress with leaded glass windows on each side,
framed by carved cypress molding. In front of the house
a wooden fence held a scattering of sheep to keep the
grass well manicured. Their white fleeces against the greenery reinforced the house's theme of white clapboard and
green shutters. The scene was both imposing and inviting.
With whoops of glee, Annabelle and Clarissa jumped from
the carriage and ran up the stairs into the house. Mandy
sat stone-still taking it all in. It was like a fairyland adventure. When the rest of the family was safely on the ground
and the baggage was being unpacked, she slowly climbed
out of the surrey and mounted the stairs, one by one.
Once inside the house, she stood in a huge hall that ran
from the front to the back. Large cypress paneled rooms
opened off the hall and a staircase—the most beautiful she
had ever seen—curved upward to the second floor. It was
connected to the wall but had no other signs of support
making it seem to be floating on air. She wandered around
aimlessly, trying to take it all in.

"Mandy! Come see the upstairs. We all have separate
rooms! Mine overlooks the side orchard. Yours is in the
back so you can see the gardens. My room is light yellow,
guess what color yours is!" Annabelle dashed halfway down
the stairs, her face flushed with excitement. Mandy smiled
and put one foot gingerly on the first step. She was almost
afraid the stairway would collapse under her weight. Carefully, she climbed to the second level. Halfway up, a large
window overlooking the back gardens lighted her ascent.
Standing in the second floor hall she gazed around in
wonder. One side of the hall contained bedrooms and an

indoor bathroom. The other side boasted a large sitting room that could be used as a small ballroom and a cozy reading room. The sleeping areas were as impressive as the main floor rooms. Carved woodwork, gilt designs on the walls, heavy oak doors, and pine floors all polished to a soft glow gave an atmosphere of opulence to even the most mundane areas. She entered Clarissa's room that overlooked part of the front entrance. Clarissa was standing beside a large window.

"I'll be the first to see Harrison when he arrives," she said, still thinking of her beau. "I have a window seat, so I can read and look out at the same time." Mandy smiled, admiring the pale peach color of the walls, and the rich multicolored cotton drapes. The room suited Clarissa. It had a sophisticated but peaceful decor. Next came Annabelle's room with its light yellow walls and moss green drapes. A small alcove with a round window offered Annabelle a place to set up an easel for painting, a talent she had just recently discovered. On one wall was a large closet in which to store all her "collections." Annabelle reveled at the spaciousness of her domain. The last bedroom was Mandy's. It was done in pale blue with darker blue and white patterned drapes. A large window with a window seat like Clarissa's allowed her to sit and meditate on the formal gardens that were just being planted. To her left she could glimpse the vegetable plot and beyond that the back of the plantation with its woods and marshes. It was a totally satisfying situation.

Three days a week, Dr. Gibbes planned to travel to Beaufort, where he shared a medical practice with an older doctor. On those days, the girls would accompany him and attend Mrs. Robeleau's Finishing School. Mrs. Robeleau was a no-nonsense teacher of Huguenot descent who was determined to stuff as much French, history, composition, and music into her students' minds as possible. It was not long before Mandy found her enthusiasm for a higher education waning as she spent most of her free time reading, writing letters or short compositions, or conversing in French. There was little time to indulge in her pastime of walking. Yet everyday brought some lesson in the natural surroundings and she felt as if she could enjoy living on a plantation forever.

Chapter Thirteen

The Gibbes had scarcely settled in before the calling cards began arriving. It seemed everyone in the area wanted to acquaint themselves with their new neighbors. Every Sunday afternoon they were invited somewhere. Mandy drank so much tea she wondered if her insides were afloat. Her sixteenth birthday came and went with little more than a family party because the first week of November both the Stuarts and the Gibbes were preoccupied with settling in. Dr. Gibbes promised her a proper celebration after the dust had settled, but Mandy assured him she was happy with the status quo. She hated being fussed over.

Mrs. Gibbes had insisted Mandy use her mother's maiden name, Greene, in the hope someone would recognize it and mention family ties. Mandy was very disappointed when Mrs. Gibbes decided to put off going to Charleston until after Christmas because she had purchased a cherry sideboard, an walnut rice bed, and other household furnishings from a widow who had decided to return to England.

"Guess what, Mandy. Our invitations to the New Year's Ball arrived today! This is the biggest and best dance of the year with the exception of the Debutantes' Cotillion." Flushed with excitement, Annabelle waved the cards in Mandy's face. "We must have new dresses for the affair. I'm old enough now to wear an off-the-shoulder gown with some décolleté." With the help of a corset, Annabelle had an hourglass figure and often stood in front of the full-length hall mirror admiring herself. Her red-gold hair, blue-grey eyes, and fair complexion turned many a young man's head.

"I've only worn my special dress twice. I doubt anyone will remember seeing it, so it will do just fine. Perhaps I can change the color of the ribbon trim," stated Mandy, who was totally uninterested in adding another frock to her wardrobe.

"You don't understand. This ball is the highlight of the year. You must look perfect. Many a match is made during this auspicious occasion. It's doubly important for us because we are newcomers and will be meeting the crème de la crème of Beaufort."

Mandy shrugged. She already had enough friends. Any more and she would flounder under her social obligations. Besides, even with all her schooling, crowds still made her nervous.

The month of December flew by in a whirl of church choir practices, dress fittings, and present making. Mrs. Gibbes insisted all the girls have totally new outfits for the dance and, as a concession to Mandy for not having a proper celebration for her birthday, insisted on paying for new shoes as well. Clarissa and Annabelle took turns teaching Mandy the dance steps that would be featured at the ball.

"You've learned to dance rather well," observed Clarissa, one afternoon as she guided Mandy in the quadrille. "Still, you're as stiff as a board. Relax. Think of yourself as a feather floating in a gentle breeze."

"I'm more a pebble in someone's shoe, than a feather in the air," groused Mandy as she stepped on Clarissa's foot during a turn. "Surely there are others like me who don't like to dance."

"Of course. But they will be at the ball, dancing. It's not a matter of like or dislike, but tradition and etiquette."

"Tradition, tradition. I'm beginning to detest that word. So far, everything I've learned at Mrs. Robeleau's has been based on tradition. A person could be plotting to poison me, but for the sake of tradition would treat me like royalty until I drew my last breath."

"Finally, you understand southern ways," laughed Clarissa. "A civilized society represses its dark side. We believe in treating people as we would like to be treated."

"Except for the slaves," thought Mandy, who did not believe in owning people.

Christmas week proved to be as chaotic in Beaufort as in Pendleton. The only peaceful moments Mandy had were those hours spent in church. She sang alto in the choir and enjoyed singing the seasonal music. This was the only place she did not mind standing next to or talking to men. It seemed natural to her to hear the beautiful blend of both men's and women's voices in song. If God had any interest in humanity at all, she thought, He would be pleased by the songs of praise offered to Him at this time of year.

Clarissa's beau, Harrison, did not visit during the holidays, a disappointment that sent her into a morose emotional state. Nothing seemed to please her, and tears flowed freely whenever things did not go her way. Mandy pondered on the power of love which could send a normally serene woman into the depths of despair. It was just another example of why not to become involved with anyone of the opposite sex, she reasoned.

The day of the ball was consumed in preparations. Everyone ate a large breakfast as it was the only complete meal they would eat that day. By mid-afternoon they had bathed and dusted themselves with scented talc—gardenia for Annabelle, jasmine for Clarissa, and rose for Mandy.

After a two-hour nap, Ruby arranged their hair; then all
the layers of undergarments were put on including their
tightly laced corsets. At this juncture the girls nibbled on
a bit of fruit to stave off their hunger pangs. Finally, they
donned their new dresses. Clarissa had selected an ivory
satin gown with gold trim; Annabelle's was a deep plum
taffeta trimmed in ecru lace; the gown Mandy wore was
of dusty rose velvet with a burgundy sash. Each girl had
dance slippers and cloaks to match her dress. They rode
to the ball in Dr. Gibbes fanciest carriage, pulled by the
team of matched greys. Annabelle talked nonstop, while
Clarissa and Mandy silently stared out the windows.

As they entered the hall where the dance was being
held Clarissa said to Mandy, "Remember, you will be
given a dance card on which your dance partners are listed.
Follow the card exactly. It guarantees that no one will feel
left out or neglected. It's tradition." She smiled wickedly.

Mandy found the ball to be similar to the one held in
Pendleton, except that everything was more intense. She
dutifully danced with everyone designated on her card.
Some were young men she had met through church or
other socials, others were older gentlemen either single or
widowed. She kept conversation going and acted interested in her partners' comments. Only her sweaty palms,
dusted with scented cornstarch and conveniently covered
by white pigskin gloves, revealed her nervousness. At the
midnight intermission, when light refreshments were
served, Annabelle sought her out.

"Are you all right, Mandy? How many times have you
been stepped on? Are you madly in love, yet?" she snick-
ered. Mandy grinned and flicked her fan wildly.

"It's just too, too much, my deah," she crooned in a
high falsetto. "The lovely ladies, handsome gentlemen,
beautiful decor, and lively music. I declare I'm about to
swoon!"

"Go ahead. I'll catch you," said a familiar deep voice behind her. Mandy whirled around, only to be face to face with Smith, who was smiling and holding out his arm.

"Oh my goodness! I'm sorry. I didn't mean to . . ."

"I agree with you. It is a bit much, but we Southerners do like to parade our assets, I'm afraid. Where else in the country could one find such an array of beautiful women? It's like being in a garden when the flowers are in full bloom—a heady experience, even for the hardest of heart. How about a breath of fresh air, or are you afraid of messing up your hairdo, which looks very becoming, by the way?"

Mandy put her gloved hand on the arm he offered and walked with him through the french doors onto the covered porch. Dampness hung in the air like a wet blanket. Too long in this humidity would definitely cause her curls to come undone.

"I must apologize for my behavior that day in Pendleton when I ran away. It was very rude," she said, anxious to get past embarrassments buried.

"Nonsense. The fault was mine. I put too much pressure on you as we had only just met. I did not realize your age or situation until Mrs. Gibbes enlightened me later. Let's forget about it. How do you like Beaufort?" Smith tactfully changed the subject.

"It is very nice. I enjoy the view of the river. There is something about water that seems to mesmerize me."

"Yes, it can be very soothing. Have you had a chance to look for your relatives, yet?"

"No. So far no one has any information, but I have not had a chance to make many contacts. I'm hoping Mrs. Gibbes will visit Charleston soon and take me with her. I'll make inquires then."

"I'm leaving for Charleston next week because father has ordered some special farm machinery, and it is ready.

I have a few connections there, relatives and such. I'll try to help you in your search."

"Thank you, Smith. I'm very grateful." Mandy could hear the musicians tuning up in the background. "I must go in. The music is about to begin. Much longer in this damp air and my hair will be as straight as a stick."

As they turned together and reentered the hall, Mandy consulted her dance card.

"I'm sorry not to be on your card," said Smith. "I was not sure I'd be coming to the ball, as I have just returned from Pendleton. Perhaps I can persuade someone to let me have a dance with you, even if I have to challenge him to a duel." Smith's eyes glittered with humor.

"Don't do anything rash on my account," returned Mandy. "My dancing is life threatening as it is. I feel like a bull in a china shop."

"That's just because you have not had the right partner."

Eventually Smith did manage a dance with Mandy. She found him to be very graceful and authoritative. With his hand on her back, controlling her movements, she matched her steps to his. The sensation was not altogether unpleasant.

At two in the morning, the party ended causing Mandy to sigh with relief. It had been a long night, and the stress of coping with so many dance partners had given her a headache.

"I'm very proud of you, Mandy," said Mrs. Gibbes as the carriage rolled along towards home. "You acted like a proper southern lady tonight."

"Thank you, Ma'am," The praise flustered Mandy, leaving her speechless.

Clarissa rode home in the silence of total disenchantment. Harrison's absence cast a pall over all the festivities for her. It was obvious no other man at the ball had captured her attention.

Annabelle, on the other hand, rattled on about first one lad then another. James was the best dancer; Garrison, the best conversationalist; Richard, the most handsome. Mandy wanted to put her hands over her ears to block out the constant prattle, but she did not want to dampen Annabelle's excitement. The plantation house was a welcome sight. Once in her room, Mandy hung up her dress then tossed everything else in a heap on a chair, climbed into bed, and was asleep in seconds.

True to his word, Smith sent out inquiries about the Drake-Greene connection while in Charleston. He returned with no conclusive evidence, but told Mandy the gossip mills were turning.

The second week of February, Mrs. Gibbes handed Mandy an envelope made of heavy manila paper with the initials CGT, embossed on the back. Mandy carefully opened it and read:

Dear Miss Greene:

I understand you are looking for relatives related to the Drakes of Charleston. Most of the family has scattered. Some are living in New Bern, North Carolina while others have moved farther West. I am the only descendent from the Nathaniel Greene side still in Charleston. If you would care to make my acquaintance please reply to the following address: 6 Glebe Street.

Miss Caroline Greene Thompson

"I must go at once to meet her," announced Mandy excitedly. "I'll just gather together a few things. . . ."

"It isn't done that way here, Mandy," interrupted Mrs. Gibbes. "You must first send a letter giving the intended day of your arrival and thanking Miss Thompson for her invitation. Then you give her time to answer back confirming your visit. She is your elder and deserves the utmost respect."

"These southern traditions will be the death of me!" fumed Mandy, yet realizing the logic of Mrs. Gibbes plan. Within the hour, she had written and posted a return letter. In it she requested a visit on March fifteenth. "Perhaps the Ides of March will be my lucky day," she mused. Within two weeks, a return letter from Miss Thompson confirmed the visit.

Jacob brought the surrey to a halt and helped Mandy down, putting her valise on the porch while Mandy knocked on the front door. The house seemed vaguely familiar to her, somehow. It was a three story brick Georgian, with a garret protruding from the roof. The front door was of cypress with a fanlight above it. An open weave brick fence with an ornate iron gate surrounded the property that consisted of several large lots. Sprawling live oaks shaded the house and the grounds.

"Miss Greene? Welcome. Please come in," said a tall, thin, middle-aged woman in a brown taffeta dress. Mandy entered a very large hall flanked by two rooms on either side. "This way. I've set tea in the parlor." Miss Thompson led the way into a spacious front room, covered from floor to ceiling in cypress panels. Tall, narrow windows allowed ample sunlight in to illuminate the area. Sterling silver plates and tea service softly shone on a low cherry table. Tapestry covered chairs and matching sofa in blue and beige scenes and a colorful oriental rug completed the decor. It was austere, yet homey.

Over a pot of Earle Grey tea and scones, Mandy shared her story. "I am the only daughter of Mary Ann Greene, who married John Cook of Knoxville, Tennessee. Mama mentioned several times she was related to the Drakes of Charleston and had a cousin Cornelia who spent the summers in Pendleton. However, Cornelia had moved to New Jersey. She was the only living relative I heard Mama ever mention. My father's family all died in a flu epidemic; he died of blood poisoning when I was only five. Then mother married Jeb Daly. He was a tyrant in every sense of the word. When she died I left him in search of kin. Now that I've found family and am almost grown I can't expect the Gibbes to continue to support me. I must become self sufficient as soon as possible."

"Don't be too hasty," said Miss Thompson, "or you will earn the reputation of being impetuous. Charleston society places women on a very high pedestal, and they are expected to comply with the custom. Women are protected and honored, first by their family, then by their husbands. If you defy tradition you will lessen your chance to marry well. I have remained single by choice, but there are many times when I have wondered if it was a wise decision. Due to the graciousness of St. Phillips Anglican Church, which has rented this property to me, and a monthly pension from my deceased grandfather, I live a satisfactory life. However, I do add to my support by tutoring students who desire to enroll in the College of Charleston. Fortunately, my family believed in educating their daughters as well as their sons. I suggest you finish your year with Mrs. Robeleau because a certificate of completion from her school will prove very influential."

Mandy choked back a sharp retort. Marriage was the last thing on her mind; nevertheless, she understood what Miss Thompson was saying. In Beaufort, one was either on top of the heap or underneath it. Her life would be much more pleasant as a member of the genteel society, rather than the working class.

"Please tell me about my family, if you can," Mandy implored. "Is it true the Drake family is somehow in my family tree?"

"Yes, several generations back. Charlestonians tend to marry their distant cousins for some reason. Perhaps they feel their blood is best, or maybe they are just too shel-

tered. There was a division among the Drake brothers
during the Revolution. One was sympathetic to the British; the other became a Charleston Whig. It was not
uncommon for families to have differing loyalties back
then, as the steady influx of immigrants guaranteed mixed
opinions. The brothers married second cousins.

The family never could resolve their differences. By
the next generation they were not even speaking to each
other, in fact, the Greene branch came into being when
Phoebe Drake defied tradition and married Nathaniel
Greene, originally from Ohio. They settled in Virginia for
a while, then returned to Beaufort where they sired several sons. Your mother came from the youngest son, James.
My mother was a Greene daughter who married William
Thompson, an enterprising Englishman. He found the
charm of Charleston irresistible and set up his business
here. We all regret the bad feelings between the relatives,
but it has gone on so long now, no one thinks much about
it. Recently, we had another family flare up over nullifi-
cation. Some of the Greenes left in a huff, moving to New
Bern. The others opted for the western frontier. It's the
Celtic blood, I think, that spawns independent thinkers
and fighting spirits. Not to change the subject, but this is
my favorite time of day to be in the garden. Let us clear
our heads by getting a breath of fresh air. We can continue this topic later."

Mandy followed Miss Thompson out the back door
into a formal boxwood garden. They meandered among
the greenery with Miss Thompson explaining the garden
lay out and the habits of each plant. It was evident she
was well-versed in botany. "I prefer to do much of the
gardening myself," she said. "I have a worker one day a
week to do the heavy labor. The rest of the time I enjoy
puttering."

Mandy smiled. The similarities between them were remarkable. She felt very compatible with this energetic, pleasant woman and was happy to have her as a relative.

By the time Jacob came the next day to take Mandy back to Beaufort, she had agreed to finish her schooling, then visit Miss Thompson again in June. In the meantime, they would correspond by letters.

Chapter Fourteen

Now that Mandy had found a relative and knew a bit about her family tree, she was able to accept herself. The change in her attitude was remarkable. Always defensive, now she became more relaxed, tempering her feisty nature with compassion and humor. She tried to find the good in every situation, even to the point where she stopped complaining about the restrictive Low Country rules.

She accepted Smith's companionship with the stipulation that they be friends only. She did not want anyone to regard her as marriage material yet because it would take time for past hurts to heal. Besides, Smith clearly preferred Pendleton to Beaufort, and she did not want to leave what little family she had found. When a function demanded she be accompanied by a gentleman, she relied on a choir member or friend of the Gibbes.

Both Clarissa and Annabelle were presented to Beaufort society at the Spring Cotillion, a coming-out ball for the blue-bloods of the city. Because of her mixed background Mandy was not eligible. Secretly she was relieved to be on the fringe of the genteel society instead of in the midst of it. Her faux pas were more forgivable.

She graduated from Mrs. Robeleau's Finishing School and received a certificate and a letter of recommendation. Now her financial situation was positive; she could teach or tutor students in French, English, history, or literature. Life was good. Her future seemed secure.

"Mandy, may I see you in the morning room for a moment?" Mrs. Gibbes asked, as Mandy finished a breakfast of fresh strawberries and cream. Clarissa and Annabelle usually slept late when they were not attending school, but Mandy always rose at dawn. She often joined Dr. and Mrs. Gibbes for breakfast, as she enjoyed listening to the doctor talk about his patients and the new advances in medicine.

Mandy followed Mrs. Gibbes into the morning room where the matron held court, answering her correspondence, planning the family menus, and scheduling activities for the servants. Often, her most intimate friends were given tea here, and it was an unstated rule that she was not to be disturbed while in this room. The soft rose walls and apple green drapes matched the floral cotton throws and rugs. It was a reflection of her personality— cool, but inviting. Now she sat at her desk while Mandy chose a carved Queen Anne chair facing her.

"I'm not sure how to begin," said Mrs. Gibbes with a gentle smile. "Please understand I do not want to hurt your feelings. You have been a wonderful addition to our family. In many ways you have been a buffer between Annabelle and Clarissa, making their lives much more balanced and interactive, without the usual sibling rivalry because they joined together to help you. And may I add you have surpassed our fondest hopes. We are very proud of you, Mandy."

Mandy smiled her thanks, wishing Mrs. Gibbes would get to the point.

"Dr. Gibbes and I have decided Clarissa and Annabelle would benefit from some time touring Europe. As you well know Clarissa is very depressed since Harrison ended his courtship, so we think a change of scenery will do her good. As for Annabelle, well, Annabelle is Annabelle, but perhaps she will gain some maturity in the study of the old masters. She has decided to pursue a vocation in art. Now that you have found a relative who seems to enjoy your company and wants you for an extended visit, we believe it would be best if you followed your heart and began to live a life of your own. We will assist you in every way we can, including giving you living expenses until you are able to support yourself. We will make sure Beaufort knows we condone your independence. You are a wise and gifted young woman. I'm sure you will be successful at whatever you chose to do."

Mandy stroked her silver cross in shocked silence. She had not considered the possibility that the Gibbes would ask her to leave. She thought she would eventually be the one to set the time of her departure amid their pleas for her continued presence. Instead, she was to be homeless again, just when she was beginning to feel secure. Oh, the irony of life! Just as Mrs. Gibbes had tried to spare her feelings, so Mandy attempted to ease the matron's anxiety at being the bearer of such surprising news.

"I was just about ready to venture forth on my own," Mandy said. "I'm sure Miss Thompson will let me help with her students until I have my own teaching facilities. I think Clarissa and Annabelle will benefit greatly from a tour of Europe as they have learned to speak French so well. I'm glad you do not expect me to go with you. I prefer to learn about my family's history here in this beautiful setting. Getting to know a city as famous as Charleston will be every bit as exciting to me as visiting Paris. I appreciate everything you have done for me. You have treated me so kindly, sparing no expense. If I have achieved anything it is because of the encouragement your family has given me. I will never be able to pay you back even if I live to be one hundred!"

"My dear, dear girl. We expect no recompense. Just follow the path God has chosen for you. That is repayment enough."

"But I don't know what God wants of me. I don't even know if He knows who I am! I'm not sure I know who He is," Mandy wanted to shout at her. She pushed the thoughts away and said instead, "When will you be leaving?"

"The middle of June. My, that is just three weeks away! We decided not to tell the girls until we had talked to you. Besides, three weeks of total confusion is enough, don't you think?"

Mandy's laughter broke the tension. "I will write to Miss Thompson today, so I will not be part of the commotion. I'll tell her to expect me in two weeks."

That evening, Dr. Gibbes held a family conference, where he told his daughters of their coming tour of Europe. Then Mandy announced her plans to spend the summer with Miss Thompson in Charleston, making it sound as if it were her own idea. The girls expressed dismay at her departure, but were so excited about going abroad that their sadness at losing Mandy was short lived.

"Rome! Paris! The paintings! The fashions! The Frenchmen! Ooo-la-la!" crooned Annabelle. "Perhaps I will spend the rest of my life in the city of love."

"I daresay you will be bored before summer ends," remarked Clarissa loftily. "I want to see London and the Shakespearean theater; perhaps go to Parliament. I would like to tell the Brits what a wonderful country they lost." Her zest for living suddenly returned. "I'm sorry you have made other plans, Mandy. Traveling abroad would be so instructive for you."

"I plan to travel around here first. Europe will have to wait. Miss Thompson has promised to take me to all the important sites. She is quite well-known, so I hope to meet the area's historians and scholars." Actually, she was more anxious to visit her relative than meet influential people, but she didn't want to seem to be playing second fiddle to the tour of Europe.

The next two weeks were filled with activity. Suddenly, none of the girls' clothes were good enough for the European scene. They plied Mandy with castoff dresses, gloves, stockings, and accessories saying they would return from Europe with trunks full of the latest fashions. Out with the old, in with the new became their slogan. Instead of one trunk, Mandy found herself with three by the time she was packed to return to Charleston. Mrs. Gibbes had given Mandy a Wedgwood tea set in a beautiful violet pattern to give to Miss Thompson as a hospitality gift. Mandy was delighted as she had little money and nothing of value to offer her cousin as a thank you for allowing her to visit.

The good-byes were short and sweet. Clarissa and Annabelle promised to come by after they had returned from their travels. Mandy thanked Dr. and Mrs. Gibbes profusely for their kindness toward her. Finally, Jacob clucked to the team and away they went. Mandy waved until a bend in the road hid the Gibbes family from her sight. As she rode along, the old familiar knot of fear threatened to constrict her breathing, but she fought it off by reminding herself that Miss Thompson was warmly anticipating her company and she was, according to Mrs. Gibbes, following the plan God had for her.

Chapter Fifteen

The June heat and humidity in Charleston proved to be stifling. Mandy soon appreciated having living quarters in the basement level of the house on Glebe Street. At least she could enjoy relatively cool nights. Sleep had never been a problem for her. Once she laid her head on the pillow she fell immediately into a deep slumber. However, in order to finish its business before the heat of the day, this city rose early. In the half light of dawn, long before the sun's first rays made their flaming appearance, the street peddlers sang out their wares, "Shrimp, fresh shrimp, penny a pound. Squash, greens, picked fresh dis mawnin'." They were better at waking her than an alarm clock.

Miss Thompson practiced healthy eating, so each day's meals consisted of fresh seafood, or lean meat, vegetables and fruit. She rarely baked sweets unless she expected company for tea. Herbs from her kitchen garden were generously used to heighten flavors. Often even the butter was seasoned with marjoram, basil, or mint. Mandy enjoyed the light fare especially on steamy days. Rice was eaten every day instead of potatoes because digesting rice did not add to body heat as did potatoes.

The social season wound down after Easter when many of the Low Country residents left for cooler, healthier climes. Mandy was concerned about earning her keep as Miss Thompson's tutoring schedule lightened.

"Dear girl, relax," commanded Miss Thompson one morning as Mandy fretted about not having enough to do. "This summer I am going to rework part of the gardens, since I have you here. Many of the perennials need dividing, and I want to enlarge the vegetable patch now that it must feed two. Since you are an expert in that field, I'm putting you in charge. Make a list of the seeds and plants you want, and I'll see you get everything. Be creative; I want to try some new items. Amos, my weekly helper will do the heavy work."

Mandy tried to remember what Dr. Adger had grown in his garden. She recalled the dark purple globe called eggplant and several varieties of melons. Perhaps they would grow here. It was too late for the cool weather plants, but she wrote down the seeds needed for the whole year so as to be prepared for fall and spring plantings. Tomatoes were particularly popular.

Miss Thompson reviewed and approved Mandy's choices, and within days everything was ready and waiting. Amos doubled the garden's size, adding rotting leaves and horse manure as compost. Mandy worked in the garden from after breakfast until noon, when the heat drove her inside. To her great delight, Miss Thompson defied tradition and refused to wear the many layers of undergarments society demanded.

"Be yourself and be comfortable," she advised Mandy. "A camisole and pantalets are enough under a day dress. You are far enough from the street and half hidden by the brickwork fence, so passersby won't notice what you have on. Besides, it is considered rude to peer into other peoples' private gardens. We'll dress formally just before the two o'clock dinner. No one comes calling until after that."

Gradually, Miss Thompson introduced Mandy to a

selection of Charleston society, most of who attended St. Phillip's Episcopal Church, where many of the city's elite worshipped. She was known for her ability to organize and was often called upon to head charitable functions. Mandy found herself helping feed the poor and working at clothing collections. She was readily accepted as Miss Thompson's niece and began receiving calling cards based on her own merit. Soon, the intricate alleys and cobblestone streets of Charleston were as familiar to her as the woodland paths in Tennessee had been. The formal gardens, blooming flowers, and raucous gulls became as enjoyable as the fields of corn and meadowlarks' song of her childhood. The charm of the Queen City completely captivated her.

"Mandy, we have been invited to Sullivan's Island to participate in a discussion of the educational needs of Charleston," Miss Thompson said one afternoon as she scanned her mail. "Several of the local tutors, including me, will meet with professors from the College of Charleston and The Citadel to examine the criteria of our educational system. I'm sure you will want to sit in on most of the meetings, but there will be ample time to acquaint yourself with island living. Just take one good dress. Everyone lets his hair down, so to speak, when on the island. There is little need for formality. That is why it is one of my favorite places."

The following Monday morning a carriage transported them to the waterfront, where a ferry took them on a delightful ride to the island. Mandy leaned over the ferry's railing to feel the cool ocean spray on her face. She wished she were going all the way to England. The rhythmic slap of the waves on the bow of the boat seemed to her a song of the deep and a promise of good things to come. Laughing children pressed her on either side as they, too, tried to get as close to the waves as safely possible. The ferry was filled with families going to and from the island. This was the morning run with a return passage leaving in the late afternoon.

Several large wooden cottages had been rented for the seminar. The men occupied one, the women, the other. From ten o'clock until two o'clock discussions about Charleston's school curriculum were held. Mandy was impressed with the wisdom her cousin displayed. She advocated educating women as thoroughly as men and pressed the group to set up schools for the children of the household slaves. Mandy was introduced as a tutor, as well as a relative, and was accepted without question. Following the mid-afternoon meal, everyone was left to his own devices.

"Miss Greene, would you care to walk along the beach? I would be happy to escort you," suggested David Lee, a teacher, one afternoon as the group dismissed. "Let us take advantage of the hard sand while the tide is out. The overcast sky is a real blessing as you will not have to worry about sunburn."

As was her custom each day on the island, Mandy headed for the beach after the meetings, eager to feel the breeze and watch the brown pelicans' antics as they dived for their dinner. Mr. Lee had spent the first two days of the session frequently glancing in her direction, so she had expected an invitation of some sort from him sooner or later. She smiled graciously and turned in the direction he pointed.

"I understand you teach several history classes at The Citadel," she said, in an attempt to keep the conversation impersonal. "How do you find the accomplishments of today's young men?"

"The men attending The Citadel are of the highest caliber physically and mentally. If they aren't when they arrive, they become so before they graduate. Lately, I have seen a renewed interest in the military exercises. I fear many lads believe there will soon be an altercation of some seriousness with our northern neighbors over the slavery issue. I understand several of the church denominations are no longer allowing pastors to rise in the church hierarchy if they own slaves. This may have some serious repercussions in the near future. Without slavery the southern economy would collapse."

Mandy had experienced enough plantation living to acknowledge this was true. "What about importing more indentured workers? Could they gradually replace the slave work force?"

"They can only be depended upon for the length of their work contract. Besides, they are too independent. Once their contracts have been fulfilled, they set themselves up in business and become our competitors. We need the security of knowing we have competent workers, who will spend a lifetime in service."

Mandy nodded. It was time to change the subject. "Look! Are those dolphins leaping in the waves? How beautiful! They are such graceful swimmers. Do you often see them here, or is this a special occasion?"

"They are common throughout the coastal region. There is a saying that when dolphins are present it is safe to go swimming, for sharks do not care to associate with them."

"Well, I am not prepared to swim, but I would like to experience wading in the ocean. Do you mind accompanying a barefoot woman, or does tradition dictate you cover your eyes?"

"Go ahead, wade. Traditions are relaxed on the islands in the summertime. If anyone of importance passes by, I'll pretend I don't know you," laughed David. "I like a young lady who knows her own mind. It makes life exciting."

"Exciting, challenging, or embarrassing; take your pick," replied Mandy, hoisting her skirt to keep the hem from getting wet. "Oh! The water feels wonderful! The sand tickles as it shifts under my toes. How refreshing!" Mandy swished her feet in the incoming surf.

They walked for about an hour. Neither was at a loss for words, and by the time they returned to the cabins they considered themselves friends.

That evening as Mandy and Miss Thompson sat on the porch enjoying the cool sea breeze and discussing the school curriculum material with the two other female tutors, Miss Thompson suggested Mandy and she take a stroll. Once out of earshot of the other ladies she said, "I understand you and David Lee did some walking this afternoon. Did you enjoy his company? I am impressed by his energy and earnestness. He comes from a prominent Charleston family, whose money originated from ship-building. David's father inherited the business, and David was expected to follow in his father's footsteps, but instead he became a teacher and historian at The Citadel. The military aspect appeals to his energetic nature, I daresay. Of course, his father was very disappointed in his choice of vocation, but there is still harmony in the family."

"It was a pleasant afternoon. His knowledge of history has made him a visionary," replied Mandy, not wanting to disclose the enjoyment she had found with David.

"Do be careful to act with all modesty and decorum. Tutors must be above suspicion in every aspect of their lives. I will be happy to act as a chaperone when you need one. We must silence the wagging tongues of the gossips before they have anything to say."

Mandy understood what Miss Thompson was trying to say. A tutor's business depended on her moral standing as well as her scholastic ability. The remaining three days of the seminar David and Mandy were careful to act above reproach. When they toured a different part of the island Miss Thompson accompanied them, occasionally turning aside to shop so the couple could talk privately from time to time. For the first time since the death of her father, Mandy felt completely at ease with a man. David proved to be courteous, intelligent, and insightful.

The final evening on the island all the members of the seminar gathered on the beach for a clambake. There was laughter, banter, singing, and storytelling around a roaring driftwood fire. Mandy found the steamed clams delicious and ate until she felt a bit queasy. David's presence next to her gave her great satisfaction, making it the perfect ending to an exhilarating week. She had come to the island as an impressionable young lady but was leaving a self-confident woman.

Chapter Sixteen

❋ ────────────────────────────────────

The remainder of the summer was spent redoing Miss Thompson's garden and formulating lesson plans for the fall tutoring sessions. Mandy's life took on a rhythm of its own, the most important aspect being Wednesday and Sunday afternoons when David came calling. With such a well-known and respected escort, Mandy visited in some of the grandest houses in the city and met many of the foremost thinkers of Charleston. As she listened to discussions on politics, agriculture, and medicine, she realized that to its inhabitants, Charleston was not just an enjoyable city, but a living history demanding to be protected, nurtured, and cherished.

One Sunday afternoon, David took her via carriage to the Magnolia Cemetery, where he pointed out the final resting places of some his ancestors and other prominent people of the city. For two hours he made history come alive as he spoke of the Pinckneys, Heywards, Draytons, and others who had helped form the fledgling thirteen colonies and develop Charleston. She learned of the two year occupation of Charleston by the British during the Revolutionary War, and of Rebecca Motte who remained in her house while it was occupied by British forces, and presided as hostess at the meals. She had hidden her attractive daughters in the attic to protect them. When the

British commander left, he looked toward the ceiling and expressed his regrets at not having met the rest of her family.

David pointed to several graves belonging to the Greene family and briefly mentioned the family turmoil. Mandy listened gravely and resolved to try to again bring honor to the Greene family name. As they returned to the carriage, David stopped, placing his hand on Mandy's arm.

"My mother would like you to come to dinner next Sunday," he said. "She has expressed her desire to meet the lady who has turned me from military strategist to a professor of local history. You will like her, I think. She is Charleston in every sense of the word, but has a fine sense of humor. The dinner will be formal as mother does nothing halfway. Wear your best finery, but don't lace your stays too tightly. Mother will insist you sample every course. I will call for you at two o'clock. Your cousin is invited, also, but it will just be a small gathering."

Mandy gave him a lopsided smile. "I'll feel like a lamb being examined for slaughter. I'm sure I will spill my wine or trip over the rug. I have butterflies in my stomach already."

"Nonsense. Just be your usual charming self. However, if I may suggest, it would be wise to keep conflicting opinions to yourself. Mother likes her dinners to radiate peace and harmony—according to her standards, of course. She is not above tossing a barbed statement or two into the conversation just to get people's reactions. Keep a cool head on your shoulders and a smile on your lips, and everything will be fine."

Mandy nodded and continued to walk toward the carriage. David's mother could hold a knife to her throat, but Mandy was determined to be the sophisticated southern lady. That night Mandy reviewed her wardrobe looking for the perfect dress. "Why should I pretend to be someone I'm not?" she said, rebelliously. "I'll wear a dress that makes a statement of who Mandy is and where she came from." She chose her royal blue dress that was made for the Valentine dance in Pendleton. After lowering the neckline and adding a large white pique collar and cuffs, she transformed it from a schoolgirl's attire to a lady's afternoon dress. She then covered a blue purse with white lace creating a matching ensemble. Her plan was to look neither regal nor rural, but somewhere in between. She wanted Mrs. Lee to know the real Mandy right from the start. If she didn't win her approval, it was best to move on before she and David became any more attached to each other. Miss Thompson pursed her lips in silent disapproval of Mandy's outfit, but guessed why her special dresses remained hanging in the closet.

As if to set an ominous beginning, a violent thunderstorm rattled the city the following Sunday. Sheets of rain poured from leaden skies. By two o'clock the streets had turned into miniature rivers. Miss Thompson's house did not have a carriage port so both of them had wet feet by the time they settled into the baroque for the ride to the Lee house, which was a half block beyond the battery, facing the Ashley River and salt marshes. As they pulled up to the front gate of the house Mandy noticed with dismay that there was no sheltered area in which to disembark at the Lee house either. It seemed Charlestonians just must ignore rainstorms. Probably the weather is beneath their dignity, she thought. Both ladies made an undignified dash through the front gate to the first floor piazza, leaving the slower moving carriage driver with the umbrella to fend for himself.

As they stood shaking the rain from their cloaks and admiring the view of the small private garden with its flowering plants and statuary, the main french doors opened and David appeared.

"Please forgive me for not personally calling for you. Mother refused to let me venture out in the driving rain. She said it would take me most of the afternoon to become presentable again and didn't want to hold dinner that long." He was dressed in a gentleman's typical summer finery—white cotton shirt, pale blue lightweight wool vest with gold buttons and watch fob, gabardine pants of a medium grey with black boots that had been spit polished. A silk ascot of blue, white, and black stripes completed his attire. Mandy had never seen him look so elegant.

As he led the way into the house, Mandy noticed the beautiful cherry woodwork that adorned the doorways, windows, and staircases. A large ornate crystal chandelier hung from a high cove in the dining room ceiling, and marble fireplaces added to the richness of the interior.

"Come in and welcome!" said a petite lady with graying auburn hair piled regally on top of her head and held with a tortoise shell comb. Her cream colored satin gown was embellished with blue embroidered silk flowers. A sapphire necklace and matching earrings added to her finery. "David, do make the introductions, so we may move on to other things. I'm sure the ladies would like a glass of refreshment after their watery trip."

David formally introduced Miss Thompson and Mandy to his mother. Mandy gave a brief curtsy, all the while searching Mrs. Lee's green eyes for signs of hostility or amusement. She found neither. Then they were ushered into the parlor where Mr. Lee and another gentleman were in a deep discussion.

"William, the ladies have arrived. Do be a dear and pick a topic of conversation we all can enjoy," cajoled Mrs. Lee as she made the introductions. Mandy found the other gentleman to be another ship builder, a Mr. Mabry. Both men wore short beards, carefully groomed and trimmed. Mr. Lee stood slightly taller than his wife; his black hair was noticeably graying at the temples. He cut a fancy figure in his afternoon fawn colored waistcoat and seal brown pants. Mr. Mabry towered over everyone in the room. He looked as if he could single-handedly lift one of the boats he built, but there was a humorous twinkle in his blue eyes, and his mouth turned up at the corners in a natural smile. His ill-fitting coat of green sharkskin suggested a man more interested in activity than fashion. Mandy was instantly at ease with him.

Since David had let it be known Mandy was interested in the history of Charleston, both men soon began to talk of some of the more colorful characters that had lived in the city such as Thomas Heyward, signer of the Declaration of Independence and good friend of George Washington. Heyward was said to have changed the words of the British national hymn "God Save the King" into the American song "My Country, 'Tis of Thee."

"Mandy, a young lady as lovely as you, was a Shakespearean actress and came to town about 1786. One of our young doctors, Joseph Ladd Brown, fell head over heels in love with her and talked of nothing else but her beauty and talent. A friend of his was not as impressed with the lady and said so. An argument ensued with the debate escalating into the newspaper in the form of letters. The ultimate end was played out in a duel where Dr. Brown was seriously injured and died three weeks later. He was only twenty-two years old. It is said his ghost still haunts the house he lived in. Let that be a lesson to you, David," said Mr. Mabry, pointedly looking in his direction. "Keep your opinions about your lady friends to yourself."

David had the good sense to look embarrassed as he said," I think Mandy would find greater benefit from hearing about some of our more illustrious Charlestonians."

"My favorite story is about Mary Weyman Brewton Foster," began Mrs. Lee. "When the British were occupying Charleston in 1781, Col. Tarleton, a pink-cheeked dandy, attended a reception where the locals spoke admiringly of the prowess of Col. William Washington, a cousin of George Washington. Tarleton said, 'I would like to see this fellow Washington of whom you people talk so much.'"

"Mrs. Foster looked him in the eye and replied, 'What a pity you did not look behind you at the battle of Cowpens.' Alas, because of her nimble wit and acid tongue, Tarleton banished her to Philadelphia. Since then we ladies have learned other ways to provoke our enemies." Mrs. Lee displayed a secretive smile.

At that point, a servant stood at the door to signify that dinner was ready. Mandy took David's arm, while Miss Thompson was escorted by Mr. Mabry. The long, cherry dining room table was graced by silver bowls of flowers and overhead, crystal chandeliers glowed with beeswax candles. Fine bone china, damask napkins, and a complete silver service at each plate bespoke the wealth of the home's occupants. For an instant, Mandy wished she had worn her finest dress. She felt a bit shabby compared to the extravaganza before her.

Dinner began with a crab bisque and miniature herbed biscuits, then came roast duckling, poached fish, sweet potato casserole, herbed green beans, rice, and shrimp gumbo, followed by fresh fruit, cheese, and coconut cake. Since Mandy had taken David's advice and not laced her corset too tightly she was able to enjoy everything. She noticed Mrs. Lee glance in her direction occasionally as she steered the conversation from one topic to another. As the dessert course arrived, so did the subtle challenge David had warned her about.

"Miss Thompson, I understand you recently took part

in the seminar for the college curriculum. As a tutor, do you not think all teachers and tutors should have advanced degrees? It seems highly unlikely a certificate for teaching is adequate for tutoring those desirous of a higher education," remarked Mrs. Lee. "Surely the psychology of teaching, taught at the university, is as important as the subject matter itself. Do you agree?"

Miss Thompson carefully placed her fork on her dessert plate. "Certainly a thorough knowledge of the subject is important," said Mandy "however, I find the talent for teaching is rarely learned, but is rather instinctive in those who are gifted with the power to teach creatively. A good teacher understands the psyche of the student, and then creates a personal teaching style suitable to that individual. One of the problems we discussed in our seminar was the theory now in practice that a general teaching method can be used advantageously for all students; the herd mentality, as it were. We are finding teachers who use that method are failing to create the kind of atmosphere that results in profound thinkers and wise counselors. I rue the day that individualism is ignored in deference to the demands of the masses. This country was founded by people seeking a safe haven for their political and religious beliefs. Although their opinions of life, liberty, and happiness were as varied as their nationalities, they were able to compromise and disagree agreeably for the good of the nation. Certainly a university education is desirable for a teacher or tutor, but the ability to transmit knowledge and stimulate creative thought is even more important. Does this seem reasonable to you all?"

"Here, here! Well said, Miss Thompson; wise teacher that you are," enthused Mr. Mabry. "I'm sure the fate of our students are in good hands if most of the instructors agree with your theory." Then, turning to Mr. Lee, he said, "William, before I go, could we look again at the wharf blueprints? Please excuse us, ladies. I certainly enjoyed your company, the delicious meal, and the stimulating conversation, but I have commitments that must be met." With a brief bow to Mrs. Lee, Mr. Mabry followed his host to the library, ending what could have developed into a heated discussion. Mandy breathed a sigh of relief and looked at David. She knew Mrs. Lee had subtly directed the remark at her lack of a college degree.

"Mother, if Miss Greene and I may also be excused, I will show her the paintings in the morning room. She has expressed an interest in our local artists." David smiled winsomely at his mother who gave him a brief nod. He was on his feet in an instant, and with Mandy by his side began to enthusiastically explain the paintings and their subjects as they left the room.

With the controversy nipped in the bud, Mrs. Lee graciously accepted defeat and became the charming hostess once again. She and Miss Thompson discussed the latest literature and the need for an expanded charity hospital.

David and Mandy eventually found themselves alone on the piazza. The torrential rain was now a fine mist. "I hope you are not upset with mother," David said, apologetically. "She does like to stir the pot of human emotions. It's just her way of seeking mental stimulation. I'm sure under the watchful eye of your cousin you will become an very competent tutor."

"Yes. I plan to act as an aide to her for a year. Then I will open my own tutorage. Perhaps I will go abroad next summer to study," Mandy said defensively. She was trying hard not to judge Mrs. Lee too harshly.

"Mandy, I would like to think that I mean more to you than just a comfortable companion and escort. In fact, I have begun to think of you in more endearing terms." David waited hopefully for her reply.

Mandy stood quietly, her gaze fixed on a flowering bush. She had not had the courage to ask herself how she felt about David, and now he was expecting an answer.

"You are more than a 'comfortable companion' as you put it. But how much more I'm not sure. I look forward to being with you and value your ideas and opinions. To say that I have completely let down my guard would not be entirely truthful. And then there is Smith LaFarge. He would like me to consider him as a suitor. However, his age and his residence in Pendleton are stumbling blocks in our relationship. Honestly, I do not want to commit to anyone just yet. For my own peace of mind, I want to develop my teaching skills. There is within me a deep need to become financially independent which, I suppose, stems from my past insecurities. Please understand I am not rejecting you, David. Quite the contrary, I seem to be baring my soul. Oh, I hope I haven't embarrassed you!"

"Not at all. I welcome the opportunity to gain some insight into your inner self. I, too, am not ready for a total commitment, as I have only been teaching for two years. Of course, father has enough money to provide me with a handsome lifestyle, but I also want to prove myself capable of being a productive citizen. At the moment, I'm happy just to know I have a small place in your heart." David reached for Mandy's hand, lifted it to his lips and gave it a quick, but firm kiss. "Mandy Greene, part of your appeal is your purposeful spirit and serious evaluation of life. It's a reminder to me that we have only a few years in which to leave this world better than we found it. Wealth and position cannot satisfy the deep inner longing we all have to live a meaningful life. Let us continue to enjoy one another's company and perhaps, one day, our destinies will intertwine."

Mandy nodded and was about to speak when Mrs. Lee stepped onto the piazza. "David, do come in and join the conversation. Your father is preaching his brand of politics to Miss Thompson, and I cannot hush him up. Perhaps you will be able to introduce another subject."

David smiled indulgently at his mother, then gently steered Mandy back into the parlor where Mr. Lee was loudly emphasizing a point. "Secession is the only answer! The South has everything in its favor to form a union of states separate from northern politics. We are a special people with a unique culture. It's time we took the reins of our own destiny!" As he stopped to wipe his brow and gather breath, David intervened.

"Father, have you told Miss Thompson of your project to introduce Welsh immigrants to Charleston? Perhaps she has some suggestions for their welfare or housing."

"Ah yes, the Welsh immigrants. Our civic club has committed to taking indentured workers from the Welsh prison system. No hardened criminals, of course, mostly tax evasion, bankruptcies, or political dissidents. Actually, it amounts to ten families. The wives and children suffer dreadfully when their men are incarcerated. We are in the process of purchasing several row houses to lease to some of them. Most of the men will be used in the ship building trade. I understand one fellow managed a large clothing store. I'm sure he will find employment in one of our local businesses. Our biggest dilemma is what to do with the women and children. It has been suggested we try to educate the adults who can't read. The small children will attend the local school. Hopefully, most of the women can work as domestics or such. If you have any suggestions. . . ."

"I will be happy to help tutor some of the women, if necessary. Perhaps Mandy could take a young lady as a tutoring project to sharpen her skills," replied Miss Thompson guardedly. "The young people should learn proper southern etiquette so as to be assimilated into our society. Not that anyone of means should take them in by mar-

riage," she added hastily. "Still, the middle class is growing, and we need to nurture its possibilities."

"Agreed," said Mr. Lee. "I shall make inquiries and
report to you later about a young woman suitable for your
purposes. Perhaps St. Phillips will adopt a family and see
to their welfare. I will contact the parish priest."

"I will abide by your decision, Mr. Lee. I think the
civic club has chosen a fine project. I wish you great success. Mandy, would you please see if our carriage has
arrived? This has been a most pleasant afternoon, but all
good times come to an end. Mrs. Lee, we thank you for
your generous and gracious hospitality. You are a credit to
Charleston society. I look forward to seeing you again."
Miss Thompson rose as Mrs. Lee rang for a servant who
brought the ladies' cloaks, now dried and brushed. David
escorted Mandy to the carriage with a promise to call on
Wednesday as usual. Then they were whisked away by the
rhythmic hoof beats of the horses.

"I'd be careful if I were you," remarked Miss Thompson as they traveled along. "Mrs. Lee is an influential
woman. I would not want her for an enemy. If your heart
is set on David, you'd best mind your p's and q's. I would
consider her remark about tutors not teaching unless they
had a university degree a veiled threat to you, brought on,
no doubt, by the fact she felt snubbed because you obvi-
ously did not dress appropriately for her dinner party. It
would be in your best interest to set aside your rebellious
nature and adapt yourself to the local culture. To be or-
nery just for the sake of individualism is foolish. If you
must draw attention to yourself let it be because of a noble
deed. Otherwise, you will discover you are not all that
different from the Mrs. Lees of the world, which may be
one reason why David is attracted to you. They say men
often marry women similar to their mothers. It's the little
boy complex, I suppose."

Mandy silently accepted Miss Thompson's advice. It was true she had unconsciously wanted to challenge Mrs. Lee to accept her, warts and all. She had not considered the fact that almost every mother believes there is not a woman on earth worthy of her son. She had acted thoughtlessly. It was to David's credit he had chosen to overlook the whole ordeal when no doubt he, too, had been embarrassed by her obvious rebellion to his family's reputation. She sighed despondently. Why did she feel the need to rebel against authority? According to Mrs. Robeleau it was the Low Country's genteel graces that had preserved its society through war and nature's havoc. Suddenly, the truth dawned on her—the dignity of one's family name was extremely important because although family members came and went, the name continued on for generations, as did people's opinion of it. The Greenes were already regarded as irresponsible by Charlestonians. She, like Miss Thompson, had the task of restoring honor to the name. It was the least she could do for her mother.

Chapter Seventeen

It was several weeks later, when to Miss Thompson's delight, St. Phillips did accept responsibility for three of the Welsh immigrants—Mr. and Mrs. Davies and their cousin, Babs Brady. They were housed in a two-story building adjacent to the church, where destitute church members stayed until their circumstances improved. When the church women hosted a tea for the three so the congregation could make their acquaintance, Mandy found herself introduced to the trio as the person who would help the ladies adjust to Low Country customs.

Mr. and Mrs. Davies, an energetic couple in their late twenties, were sponsored by a member of the civic club who managed a hotel in the city. The immigrants were expected to work there for two years to pay their passage expenses. They looked more than adequate for their tasks as they were short, brawny, and glowing with good health. Wide smiles and musical laughter added to their appeal.

Babs was a totally captivating 12-year-old who had a mop of fiery red curly hair and bright blue eyes that shone with joy and enthusiasm. Her voice had such a lilt that Mandy wasn't sure if she was singing or speaking. Her hands moved to and fro as she spoke and her restless feet seemed to be keeping time to an inner rhythm. She was just emerging into womanhood, but promised to be a

beauty once she passed the awkward stage. All three spoke
English, but with a heavy Gaelic accent that caused Mandy
to guess at half the words they were saying. Their open,
unveiled zest for living was refreshing, and Mandy could
hardly wait to begin her work as tutor. She made arrangements to meet the ladies the following Tuesday to walk
them to Miss Thompson's house where their lessons would
be taught. Mrs. Davies could stay only until noon because
of her work at the hotel, but Babs would continue on until
two o'clock, as she was needed later to clean up after the
hotel's dinner hour.

"Where should I start? I need a plan that will benefit
them both so they will not feel so self-conscious," Mandy
asked her cousin one evening as she worked on lesson
plans.

"First things first," Miss Thompson replied. "Teach
them the meaning of some of our local words and phrases.
Remember how confused you were when we told you to
mash the doorknocker or redd-up your room? If they
understand the meaning of what we are saying they will
be more at ease. You must also teach them how to interact
in our society. The sooner they begin to practice Low
Country ways, the easier it will be on everyone."

Mandy nodded as she prepared a list of questions she
wanted to ask them. Being a tutor was going to be very
educational.

Tuesday morning Mandy could hardly eat breakfast
because of her nervous stomach. She dressed in a simple
day dress and wore only her mother's silver cross as jew-
elry because she wanted to identify with them on their
level. The memory of the outmoded, oversized black dress
she wore while traveling was still fresh in her mind. The
walk from Glebe Street to St. Phillips took only a few
minutes in the pleasant morning air. As she entered the
parish home, the two women were waiting for her in the
lobby.

"A grand mornin' to ye," greeted Mrs. Davies, smiling. "We'll not be detainin' ye. Babs has had me up since the crack o'dawn lest ye come earlier than expected."

"God bless ye, Mistress Greene," chimed Babs, giving Mandy a quick curtsy. "We've gotten a start already by listenin' to the folk who live here. Tis a wee bit confusin', but we're muddlin' through. I 'ave some questions for ye when we get to studyin'."

"I can see you both are eager to begin. Follow me and take notice of the turns and street names. Tomorrow you will be expected to come on your own." Mandy glanced at the frayed wool dresses they wore and made a mental note of their sizes so she could search for clothing more suitable.

As they climbed the entry stairs at 6 Glebe, the women fell silent, overcome by the size and impressive architecture of the house. Mandy led them directly to her study room and motioned for them to sit on the ladder back chairs placed around a maple table.

"You have come to an area of the United States that has its own peculiar customs and mannerisms. This week we will discuss them, so you will be able to function more competently at the hotel and among the local people." While speaking, Mandy passed paper and pen to them. Soon they were in a lively discussion of when to curtsy, whom to introduce first, and when a chaperone is required. Before they knew it, the bells of St. Michael's church were announcing the noon hour. Mrs. Davies hastily put her studies aside.

"I don't want to be late for me job," she said, hurrying to the door. "I will come again on Thursday. Thank 'ee, Miss Greene." With a bob of her head, she slipped out and headed in the direction of the hotel.

"Goodness, the morning has gone by so quickly. Would you care for a cup of tea?" asked Mandy.

"I'd be much obliged," said Babs. "I was so excited about me lessons, I couldn't stomach much food this mornin'."

Mandy smiled. So she wasn't the only one who had suffered apprehension about the schooling. She decided this would be a good time to become better acquainted with the radiant girl in front of her. "Tell me about yourself," she requested as she brewed the tea. "That is, if you feel comfortable talking about your past. I surely do not want you to bring up bad memories."

"Oh no, miss. Most of me memories are passable. I grew up on a small farm in Wales. I was one of thirteen children including two sets of twins. Me pa farmed and worked as a carpenter. He was a patient man who didn't take to drink. 'Course he liked a pint now and again, but he was responsible to his family. Me mum was a jolly soul, always singing and laughing. A lively one, she was. But when the last babe came, she had complications and died in childbirth. Me pa went kinda crazy for a while; his way o' grieving, I suspect. We children tried to keep house and family together, but pa felt overwhelmed. Before we knew it, the young babes had been given to folks in the neighborhood who were childless; the older boys hired on as sailors, and the older girls given jobs as household help. I was lucky. Harry and Emily Davies took me in. I often visited them so they knew me quite well. I was to help when Emily had her baby but, God love her, she lost the babe in the seventh month; stillborn it was. She was heartbroken. Harry's job as a store clerk petered out about the same time. What little money they had saved was used to pay the doctor. They had no close relatives and probably would have ended up in debtor's prison when word came of work in America. They sold everything, used most of the money to bribe a prison clerk to include them in the lot that was coming and here we are. . . ." Babs took a deep drink of her tea before continuing. "Me mum had a strong faith and taught us to look to the Lord. God loves us, and with Him in charge things always turn out for the best, she said."

"Hmmmm, That is one way of looking at life. I can see your optimism in your eyes. It is very becoming to you."

"Yes, miss. Me faith is strong like me mum's was."

"Well, if you've finished your tea, I'd like to have you read to me, so I can see just what kind of a scholar I am teaching." Mandy handed Babs a fourth grade reader, the first of several books each more difficult than the other. Babs sailed through several pages before Mandy stopped her.

"Your reading is excellent, but we pronounce some of the words differently. Listen as I read page five." By the time two o'clock came, Mandy and Babs were deep into a discussion of British history. Mandy was disappointed to have to tear herself away from this bright, vivacious young girl.

"I will expect you at the same time tomorrow. We will continue where we stopped today, although I will revise my lesson plans to accommodate your reading level. I am amazed you are so competent with what little formal teaching you have had. Your parents are to be commended."

"Me pa read to us often in the evenings, and mum made us memorize Bible passages. The other books I read came from me grandpa's book collection which was willed to us." Babs smiled her thank you, curtsied, and hurried off to the hotel.

Mandy returned to the table and began a new outline. "I've met my match," she said to herself. "Babs is moving through the same situations I did several years ago, although she has the Davies for support. Perhaps that is why she is so joyful and confident." Yet even as she thought on this she realized Babs' joy had an inner origin unknown to herself.

The next several weeks passed as if in a dream. Mandy continued to stress to the two immigrants the importance of embracing Low Country traditions, and they became proficient in the social graces. She had asked her cousin to find the ladies several day dresses, and was pleasantly surprised when Miss Thompson's garden club supplied not only dresses but underwear, shoes, and accessories. Now Babs and Mrs. Davies looked like Charlestonians, that is, until they opened their mouths. Both continued to speak with strong Welsh accents, causing Mandy to reflect on the strange coincidences of life. Annabelle and Clarissa had to cross the ocean to get a taste of European culture while a bit of Wales came right to Mandy's doorstep.

The third week of September an unfamiliar tread was heard coming up the front steps. In answer to the insistent knocking, Mandy opened the door and gasped with surprise. "Smith! How nice to see you! What are you doing here? Please come in." Mandy led the way to the parlor that glowed softly with the rays of the setting sun. She quickly lit several candles. "Do sit down and tell me all the news of Pendleton. I hope no unhappy situation has brought you back home."

"I'm here because my grandmother is failing. I love the grand old lady and came for a final visit. The family will miss her wit and no-nonsense attitude. She has a heart of gold."

"I'm so sorry. I rather envy you having a grandmother. I am happy here with Cousin Caroline, but I wish I could meet other family members. Most of them are genteel rascals from what I understand. Are you happy in Pendleton? Do you ever see the Synnes or some of my church friends? How is your cotton crop coming along?"

As the twilight deepened casting purple shadows around the two friends, Smith told Mandy everything of interest about Pendleton that he could remember. Mandy sat spellbound, partly because of his stories and partly because she had never seen him looking so attractive. The summer sun had bronzed his features and lightened his hair. He spoke like the plantation overseer he was, with optimism, enthusiasm, and insight. A pulsing desire for him began deep within her. For the first time in her life she wanted a man's arms to enfold her, holding her close. She looked deeply into his eyes and saw there a desire that matched her own. A thousand unspoken words passed between them, the air fairly crackling with the electricity of restrained passion. Then, as quickly as it had risen, it vaporized, as Miss Thompson, returning from a church meeting, entered the room.

"I thought I heard a man's voice," she remarked, smiling at Smith briefly before scolding Mandy with a look. "Mandy, where are your manners? A lady never entertains a gentleman without a chaperone present. Mr. LaFarge, I do apologize for my wayward cousin."

Smith laughed gently. "I'm afraid the fault is mine, ma'am. I arrived without notice, putting Miss Mandy in a tizzy. She was so anxious to hear news of her former home she forgot all about the niceties. But now that you are here, I will proceed with my progress report." Smith continued his tales of Pendleton. It was evident he now considered that area his home. He was in the process of enlarging the farmhouse and building a stable and carriage house. The cotton was thriving, and he had joined the farmers' association.

"I will be in Beaufort for several weeks, Miss Thompson. May I ask your permission to walk out with Miss Mandy? It seems in my absence she has evolved into a charming southern belle."

"You may visit after the dinner hour. Mandy has classes in the morning. If a tour of the city or countryside is imminent, I shall make arrangements for others to accompany you, as my schedule does not permit many extra curricular activities."

"That seems reasonable," replied Smith. "I would like Mandy to visit my family in Beaufort on Saturday, next. It is my sister's twenty-first birthday, and we are planning a surprise party for her. Of course you are expected, also, Miss Thompson." Smith deferred to her politely, then turned to Mandy. "Tiffany, my sister, is somewhat of a tomboy. If you plan to bring a gift she would much prefer an unusual plant to any feminine bauble. I think she has more of a planter's disposition than I. She is constantly outside tending her gardens or riding through the fields."

Mandy decided she liked Tiffany already. She looked at her cousin for a conformation of the invitation, but Miss Thompson had a slight frown on her face. "What accommodations do you propose for us?" she asked. "I fear the drive to Beaufort and back in one day would be too much for me."

"Our plantation house includes several guest wings. You would be expected to occupy one of them. They are charming and peaceful and would provide a time of relaxation for you. I notice you have rather extensive plantings; I would encourage you to come see Tiffany's gardens. She recently had some exotic plants sent to her from China."

The mention of rare botanicals piqued Miss Thompson's curiosity. She nodded, saying she would give the invitation serious consideration. Smith thanked her and prepared to leave.

"May I call on Mandy Thursday? I would like to take her for a drive along the Ashley River. I will provide a proper chaperone for the occasion as my Aunt Bess wants to do some shopping here in the morning. I will come for Mandy at two."

"That will be fine, weather permitting," Miss Thompson said as she extinguished one of the reading candles, indicating it was time for Smith to depart. He cast a meaningful look at Mandy and walked out the front door.

That night, Mandy lay sleepless on her bed, mulling over her sudden surge of emotion brought on by Smith's visit. Was she in love? Perhaps it was just the news of her friends in Pendleton that had brought on the excitement. Yet when she closed her eyes, Smith's face, so full of longing and passion, filled her imagination. She stirred restlessly as her heart raced in response to his unspoken entreaty.

The following day, Mrs. Davies and Babs arrived late, breathless with excitement. "I've never seen the like of it since coming to America!" exclaimed Mrs. Davies. "Babs held the feverish babe in her arms and said a simple prayer. Then, in front of us all, the fever left the child's system. Went right down her body and out her feet. We could see her normal color return and hear her raspy breathing clear. It was a miracle! An honest-to-goodness miracle!"

Babs stood with a wide smile on her face, her eyes shining. "'Tis the love o'Jesus that healed that babe. Och, how He loves the wee ones!"

Mandy stared at them with disbelief. She had never heard of such a thing. The parish priest inferred the age of Bible miracles was past. She had heard of several episodes while in Pendleton where God had seemingly intervened in sick people's lives, but she had dismissed them as coincidence. "Has this happened before when you've prayed?" she asked Babs.

"'Tis the first for me, but me mum had the Spirit's gift o'healing. She would lay hands on sick people, and many times they would get right up from their beds, completely well. Sometimes the healing was gradual, but mum said when Jesus prayed over sick folks the healing came right then, and we were to expect the same. She always prayed for us children. We were rarely ever ill."

"But she died an untimely death. Could she not pray for herself? Did God's healing power not extend to her?"

"'Tis a mystery, to be sure. I think my pa asked himself the same questions. Perhaps that was why he went a bit balmy. His wife, who prayed for many to be healed, died at an early age. But mum had told us not to question God's ways. One of the Scriptures she had me memorize says, 'The righteous perisheth, and no man layeth it to heart: and merciful men are taken away, none considering that the righteous is taken away from the evil to come' (Isa. 57:1). I found peace by thinking on that. Me mum is at rest. Her trials are over. It's the rest of us who must struggle on. That's one o'the benefits of believing in Jesus as Savior: our fear o'death is gone because we know for certain we are kept in His love as we wait for His return."

"Return?" Mandy looked bewildered. "God is coming back? Whatever for?"

"For us, of course. To take us to our heavenly home, the New Jerusalem."

"I've never considered such an event. I'm sure I have never heard the priest mention such a place. I thought the prayer book was the only comfort we had; it's filled with good thoughts."

"Jesus says you must be born again, or you will never see heaven. He means you must have a personal relationship with Him that goes beyond the prayer book or the sermons of the priest. Even good works such as your cousin so often does will not provide her with eternal life. Jesus wants us to believe in Him and talk to Him in our own words because He created us and desires our friendship. Besides, He is the only one who can forgive our sin, so we can become children of God. God is too holy to claim us until we are cleansed of sin by Jesus. That is the meaning of the cross you wear."

"Well, you seem to know a lot for a 12-year-old sprite," Mandy said, a bit resentfully. She was the teacher, but where was her understanding of God? This girl with the blazing blue eyes was so sure of her relationship with Him, she put Mandy on the defensive. "You've given me much to think about. Now, why don't we settle down to our lessons. I believe you both were to write compositions. Mrs. Davies, would you please read yours?"

While Mrs. Davies' voice droned on, Mandy thought about the baby's healing. What was the real explanation? People were fickle. They tended to believe anything, given the proper atmosphere. She knew her mother had believed in God, but had God cared about her? Was her death God's will, a rescue from her dire straits? Was it meant to be?

There was silence in the room when Mrs. Davies finished reading. Mandy was totally absorbed in her thoughts. A gentle cough from Babs jolted her back to reality. "That was fine, Mrs. Davies," she murmured, reaching for the lady's paper. "I'll correct the grammar after Babs reads her paper."

Babs had written about the trip to America—the storms at sea, the seasick passengers, the grumpy captain. Mandy tried to concentrate. "You should say berths were, not was; Mrs. Davies and I, not me; remember, use my when it's possessive—my dress, my hair, my cousin."

Babs struggled on, trying to correct her grammar as she read, but somehow it all fell flat. "I'm sorry, Mistress Greene. Me, uh, my thoughts just aren't on my studies. As my mum, or rather, mother would say, I'm too heavenly minded today to be any earthly good. If I was at home, we'd be praising God for His healing mercies and dancing 'round the room for joy. Our religion never was the stuffy kind. We've always had a holy joy."

Holy joy! Something within Mandy stirred. That's

what set Babs apart. It was joy, a holy joy. Suddenly her eyes filled with tears, and a lump rose in her throat. Oh, how she wanted that joy and the freedom to love! She turned her back to them pretending to search for something on her desk until she had regained control of herself. "It's almost noon. Why don't we dismiss a bit early? Tomorrow we will review the history of the Revolutionary War. Read chapter six in your history book." With a forced smile she waited while they gathered their books and cloaks, then walked them to the door. Closing it firmly behind them, Mandy leaned against the unyielding wood, letting the tears flow freely down her face. "Oh, God! I want the joy and faith Babs has! How do I find You? I want to know You! If You can really forgive sin, Jesus, forgive mine! Tell me You love me; I need someone to love me!"

Sobbing, she slid down the door until she was sitting in a heap on the floor. It seemed her tears came from the depths of her being in a never-ending stream. But it was a healing flow, for when her sobs turned to gentle gasps there was a lightness in her spirit that had never been there before. An invisible presence seemed to fill the room, flooding it with peace. She felt comforted, as if she were being cradled in arms of love. She closed her eyes and surrendered to the divine presence surrounding her.

Chapter Eighteen

A fresh new wind was blowing. It was the wind of God's spirit, and it was blowing new life into Mandy. First came the peace of knowing God loved her. He had washed her clean within, making even her body seem holy and acceptable to her. Then, there was the peace of knowing she belonged to Him. Even her face reflected her new experience—her expression had softened, giving her an almost ethereal look. Her mind seemed to hover between heaven and earth, making it difficult to concentrate on mundane matters. She read Scripture every chance she could. Passages seemed to leap from the pages and burn themselves into her soul.

When Smith came on Thursday to take her on a picnic he noticed the difference in her immediately. The wary, haunted look in her eyes had been replaced by the glow of deep contentment. Her voice was softer and kinder, somehow, making her even more womanly and appealing. His Aunt Bess, acting as chaperone, was attracted to Mandy immediately.

The weather cooperated by changing from the high humidity of summer to the drier, cooler air of autumn. Migrating birds by the hundreds were seen on the marshes as the trio rode along the Ashley River. Smith's high stepping Saddlebreds pulled the surrey with ease. Soon they entered the long, oak-lined lane leading to a large plantation house.

"What a beautiful place," remarked Mandy, as they walked along a canal which fed the rice fields that stretched in every direction. Smith found a level grassy spot along the riverbank, and there they spread the picnic fare. Mandy looked around, overcome by the beauty of nature. A hymn of praise to her Creator rose within her.

"Tell me your thoughts," prompted Smith, noticing the rapt look on her face.

"I was just thinking how nature displays the greatness of God. I remember reading a Bible verse that said, 'The Lord by wisdom hath founded the earth; by understanding hath he established the heavens. Proverbs 3:19, I think."

"This country could surely use some of His wisdom, what with all the talk of secession," observed Smith wryly. "Some of the men of Pendleton are secretly meeting. I believe they are beginning to stockpile weapons. What will happen to our crops if we concentrate on war instead of agriculture? I want no part in it." He passed Mandy a plate of fried chicken. "Well, we did not come here to talk politics. Aunt Bess, this rice salad is delicious! Would you please slice me a large helping of that sugar cake? Thank you."

Sugar cake! Suddenly Mandy remembered her desire to live in a fancy house and have sugar cake every day. Her fantasy was coming true! The house she called home was amazingly like the one in her dream; and now she was eating sugar cake. She took a small bite and let it dissolve in her mouth. Mmmmm! To her it was like the manna God gave Israel in the desert. How good her life was now. It seemed all the struggles were over. If only.....

"Mandy! Where are you? I asked if you had heard from Clarissa and Annabelle since they arrived home." Smith seemed a bit annoyed by her inattention.

"I'm so sorry! I was daydreaming. It must be the peaceful atmosphere. Yes, they sent a letter last week saying they had a wonderful time in Europe. Clarissa was introduced to a duke or baron or some titled person, and they are now corresponding regularly. Annabelle fell in love with the artists' community of Paris and plans to return there next summer. They have asked me to come visit on my birthday, so I shall make it an extended weekend, as I do not want to be away from my students for very long."

"You seem to be putting down deep roots in Charleston. Do you ever wish to live again in Pendleton? The climate there is so refreshing and it is such a progressive town. The railroad is expected in another year or so."

"Pendleton is very dear to me," Mandy said hesitantly, trying to avoid hurting Smith's feelings. "Had it not been for that lovely town I would not be here today. However, Charleston is where I feel at home. Cousin Caroline has been like a mother to me—guiding, correcting, and encouraging. I think I fill a gap in her life, too."

"But what about your future? What are your aspirations and desires?"

"Smith, in a few weeks I will be seventeen. I have no desire at this time to be anything other than an excellent tutor. The rest I leave in God's capable hands. He knows best."

At this point, Aunt Bess, who had been quietly reading, murmured something about a particular flower she wanted to examine and left the couple to their private conversation. Smith grabbed Mandy's hand and held it tightly.

"Something about you is different. Your restless spirit has been subdued, making you seem so content and peaceful. Your whole nature has softened. What has happened to you? Surely this is something that goes beyond Miss Thompson's influence."

"I'm not sure how to say this, Smith. I know you go to church regularly and believe in God, but I was never sure who God was until recently when I gave myself to His Son, Jesus Christ. He has transformed me. For the first time, since the death of my mother, I know I am loved, deeply loved, and that I belong to Someone I can trust with every aspect of my future. I no longer have any desire to steer my own course in life because my destiny is in God's hands. I am at peace."

Smith sat speechless, staring at Mandy. "You are not planning to enter a nunnery, are you?"

"Of course not, but all of a sudden life seems so full of possibilities. Before, I carried so much emotional baggage I could not see my own potential. Now that I'm free of that, I've just begun to discover the real me, and I like what I see. I no longer have to hide behind family or friends because my identity comes not through another human being but through Christ. Forgive me, I am not explaining things too well. It is all so new to me. . . ." Mandy's voice trailed away.

"Well, whatever has happened, I find you a much better person in every way. I'm happy for you, but I suspect I shall go back to Pendleton without a commitment from you. I shall be old and gray before you consent to wed me, I fear." Smith gave a halfhearted laugh, but Mandy saw the hurt in his eyes.

"Dear Smith, I am very fond of you, but you would have gone back without a promise from me regardless of my spiritual condition. I know many young ladies consider themselves ready for marriage at my age, but I am not one of them. I do not crave the security and social amenities of married life. I want to try my wings and fulfill my goals before I become a matron. I'll admit I find you terribly attractive and a man of great potential, but it will be some time yet before I pledge myself to another."

"Ah, Mandy, how you trifle with my affections. Well, I shall be back in December for the social season. I warn you, I will wage an all-out campaign to win your heart. But for now, we had better return to the city before darkness obscures the road. I will see to Aunt Bess, if you will pack up our leftovers." Smith ambled off in the direction his aunt had taken, while Mandy hastily placed the remaining food and utensils in the hamper then shook and folded the blanket. The joy she had felt was now obscured by a cloud of sadness at having to deny Smith her hand in marriage. Perhaps she should advise him to seek a wife elsewhere, but there was a feeling of pride within her knowing she was the object of his affection. Maybe by Christmas she would feel differently, especially if he would agree to a long engagement.

Conversation was nil on the way back to Charleston. Aunt Bess tried to introduce several topics of interest, but met with little success. Mandy and Smith answered her questions politely, but each was preoccupied with other thoughts.

"How glad I am to be past the anguish of first love," Bess thought, remembering her own stormy courtship. Now her children were grown, and her husband was involved with plantation problems and ill health. She wished she could make them understand how quickly life passes. She had been a productive person and was satisfied with her marriage, but she knew others in difficult situations who could hardly wait for death to release them from their misery. She decided it was best to let Smith and Mandy resolve their own differences.

"Thank you, Smith, for a lovely picnic. It was wonderful to visit the countryside." Mandy smiled gently and gave his arm a squeeze as he helped her down from the carriage.

"The pleasure was all mine. I will count the days until I see you again."

Mandy turned quickly and entered the house before his manly presence overcame her resolve. As she entered the parlor Miss Thompson was lighting the lamps. "Cousin Caroline, a cup of tea would taste good. Will you join me?"

Miss Thompson nodded and set out the tea service while Mandy heated the water. The soothing warmth of the brew soon dissolved Mandy's tension. "Forgive my impudence, but why did you not marry? An elegant, well-traveled woman like you are, must have had a passel of suitors from which to choose. Smith is pressing me for a commitment, but I am not ready for so great an obligation. Am I making a mistake?"

"My dear, the very fact you are hesitant proves you are not ready for marriage. Keep a cool head on your shoulders. Many young women confuse love with lust and allow their passions to influence their decisions, resulting in a lifetime of regret or loneliness. Marriage is not to be rushed into for God considers the marriage covenant unbreakable. 'Til death us do part' are not just words to be said, but a promise to keep.

"As for me, I have always had a rather distant personality. Added to that was my love for traveling, which my father encouraged. His business was international, and he enjoyed my acting as traveling companion and hostess to his associates as my mother had other interests. I'm afraid I seemed rather unapproachable to many of the young men of my time. However, I met a man in Scotland who swept me off my feet. He was everything I ever wanted in a husband—intelligent, thoughtful, curious, and jolly. We were compatible in every way. He was on his way to visit me in Charleston and meet my family, when he was taken ill with a fever and died at sea. I spent two years grieving my loss. By the time I felt ready to socialize again all the suitable men of my generation were taken. I refused to marry just for the sake of changing my name or for security, and I was not interested in men twice my age. I began teaching and found I had an aptitude for it. Instead of raising my own children, I discovered I could influence the many students who came to me for help. I take great satisfaction seeing them graduate from college and become useful citizens. I am very grateful for my life as it is for I believe I am in God's will."

Mandy held the warm teacup between her hands. "That is also my desire, and I pray about it daily, to find and follow the path God has for me. But how can I be sure I'm in His will? There seems to be several options open to me."

"God hears your prayers, and He will give you both the desire and the aptitude for the work He plans you to do. Worry will only hinder your ability to hear His voice. Do whatever brings you peace. If you stray from His path, the Holy Spirit will gently convict you. Think of God as a loving Father, not a stern taskmaster."

Both ladies sat in the soft glow of the lamps lost in thought; Mandy was searching for her future, Miss Thompson reliving her past.

Chapter Nineteen

Mandy carefully selected her clothes for the visit to the LaFarge plantation as she did not want a repeat of her rudeness at the Lee house. Into her trunk went two special occasion dresses and several of her best day dresses. If Tiffany was the outdoor enthusiast Smith claimed her to be, perhaps they would do some hiking. Mandy packed a pair of comfortable walking shoes along with several pair of dress shoes.

The LaFarge rice plantation was located between Charleston and Beaufort on the Combahee River. It was one of three plantations owned by the LaFarge family. The plantations were situated about fifteen miles inland as the first ten miles of river water was too salty to grow rice. By the 1850s, twenty-two families grew 40 percent of the rice, called Carolina gold. The yearly rice harvest was about ten million pounds. Most of the slaves who worked the rice came from Sierra Leone, Africa, where they had grown up tending rice fields. Because of their previous experience they did all the work, flooding the fields, draining, planting, and harvesting. During the off-season they repaired dikes and canals and cleared additional land of the mighty cypress trees, so more rice could be planted. The threat of yellow fever and malaria carried by mosquitoes caused the white plantation families to leave their farms in April, to go to the barrier islands or the mountains, where they remained until after the first hard frost, usually in November. Since the slaves were more resistant to the diseases, they managed the crops on their own. This year there had been an early killing frost thus allowing the LaFarge family to return to their plantation in late October.

Miss Thompson thoroughly enjoyed the carriage ride as she had not been outside the Charleston area for some time. As they approached the LaFarge fields, she pointed to a group of white cattle with humps on their backs grazing among the trees. "I haven't seen Brahman cattle for years. They are imported from India and are especially suited to our hot, humid climate where they are often crossbred with our local breeds. Mr. LaFarge must be a very progressive farmer."

The winding lane to the house was shaded by the usual live oaks, but under these spreading trees had been planted shrubs of every description adding background texture to the multicolored granite statues nestled in the greenery. The effect was striking.

"I wonder if that is Tiffany's doing?" remarked Mandy, pointing to a large statue of Pan playing his flute. A sudden turn revealed a huge reflection pond in front of a large, columned mansion on a small hill. Surrounding it on all sides were boxwood mazes and meditation gardens replete with more statuary.

"Well! It was worth the trip just to see this. I hope my offering of cuttings and graftings will not seem insignificant." Miss Thompson had brought samples of many of her exotic plants as her gift to Tiffany.

"Look! The slave cabins are arranged like a miniature town square with vegetable gardens and flowers beside each cabin. Everything is so well kept. These must be God-fearing people." Mandy had never seen such tidy grounds.

As the carriage drew up to the front door, Smith bounded down the steps. "Good morning! I trust the ride was pleasant. Joseph will take your trunks, while I direct you to your suite." He helped Miss Thompson down first then, brazenly holding Mandy by the waist, swung her lightly over the side of the carriage. "Just as I thought, you are as light as a zephyr and as welcome." He held her hand for a minute then led them to a side wing of the house that had its own entrance half hidden by a formal English garden. "The frost killed most of the flowers, but I hope you will enjoy those remaining. Feel free to walk in any of the gardens, but be careful in the mazes as it is very easy to become disoriented."

"The grounds are gorgeous! Is it all Tiffany's doing?" Mandy could hardly believe one person could be so creative.

"Tiffany's and about twenty gardeners. She gets many of her ideas from gardening magazines that are sent her from abroad. By the way, don't mention her birthday. I told her I had invited you as weekend guests so Mother could meet you."

As they entered the wing, Mandy had a hard time keeping a look of astonishment from her face. Marble tiles of various colors had been used throughout the suite. Mandy's room was in pink polished marble while Miss Thompson's room shimmered in pale green and white. The floors were covered with black marble that had gold streaks running through it. Gold adorned the chandeliers, doorknobs, and fireplace utensils. Flowers in gold vases graced every room, and in the parlor a budgie cooed a welcome from a golden cage.

"I will leave you to freshen up. When you are ready to socialize, use this tapestry bell pull and one of the servants will escort you to the main house for tea. Dinner is at three, so you will have ample time to change before then.

I will see you soon." Smith smiled and gently closed the door behind him.

"Well, I never! I don't believe even the king of England lives in such luxurious accommodations," murmured Miss Thompson. "This is almost beyond belief."

Mandy touched a tile surrounding the fireplace. It was hand painted and depicted a particular flower. Every tile represented a different flower, and the outer row boasted ivy running wildly up toward the mantle mirror. Floor to ceiling windows of leaded glass with beveled edges refracted the sunlight creating dancing rainbows on the walls. The canopied beds were fluffy with down quilts, causing Mandy to plop herself down and groan with delight.

After a brief rest and change of clothes Miss Thompson declared herself ready to join the other guests. Mandy tugged at the bell pull and within a minute or two a uniformed servant appeared at the door to escort them to the main parlor where a light fare of finger food and beverages had been prepared. Smith was waiting for them.

"Ladies, how lovely you look. No one would suspect you had been on the road for hours. May I present my mother, Mrs. Corrine LaFarge." Mrs. LaFarge was a stout woman with a mass of dark brown hair and liquid brown eyes. Although plain of face, her fashionable wardrobe and erect bearing gave her a queenly appearance. Mandy curtsied and spoke the customary greeting. Miss Thompson addressed her in French, which delighted the hostess so much she immediately invited her to a corner of the room for an intimate chat.

"Well, look at that," said Smith. "How convenient. Let me show you the special features of the house, while the ladies are conversing." They wandered from one elegant room to the next. Paintings by European artists, ornate silver bowls, and crystal chandeliers emphasized the wealth of the owners. It looked more like a museum than a house to be lived in by one family. The stairs leading to the second floor had a double curve with a large window at the halfway point. Featured on the second floor was the ballroom filled with fresh flowers. Servants were scurrying everywhere setting up a long table at one end of the room.

"We will have the birthday party in here," Smith said. "Everything is to be finished by two, then we will lock the doors until the reception at eight-thirty. Tiffany knows nothing about this. She expects only a fancy dinner this afternoon. I'm sorry she was not here to greet you, but she has gone riding with some of her friends and won't be back until two o'clock. I suppose you think that is rude, but Tiffany has a mind of her own. In the meantime, we are free to explore her gardens. However, since so many of them are high mazes I think we had better be accompanied by Miss Thompson. I wouldn't want to ruin your reputation." Smith put his arm around Mandy's waist and pulled her close.

"Nor I, yours," replied Mandy, taking a step away from the scent of his manly body. It was time to change the subject. "I can't get over the size of the house. How many servants do you have to attend to everything?"

"We have thirty household servants, twenty for the grounds, and several hundred to work the rice. Father buys only the best people and often pays over a thousand dollars for one healthy male. The other two plantations have an equal number of field hands, but since there are no large houses on the properties, no household help is needed other than what is necessary for the comfort of the overseer. Father is a progressive planter and tries the latest methods and equipment, but nothing can get rid of the stench of the stagnant water when the rice is growing. I can't stand that smell or the bugs that pester the life out of all living flesh. That is why I talked him into buying a cotton farm in Pendleton. The air is so much sweeter there, I feel healthier than I have in years."

Mandy gently steered Smith in the direction of the parlor to rejoin the other guests. As he mingled with friends, she filled a small plate with several sandwiches, took a cup of tea, and sat where she could see the rose garden and the fields beyond. Could she manage the servants on a large enterprise like this? Is this what God had in mind for her? A plantation wife had as much responsibility as her husband but in different ways. The man was concerned with the laborers and crops; the woman had to handle all the domestic problems, nurse the sick—both black and white, bear children, and entertain. It was a daunting lifestyle. She wasn't sure she was up to its rigorous demands.

At two o'clock the tea ended, and the guests retired to their rooms to rest and dress for the formal dinner. Mandy was glad for the break as she still found making conversation taxing. She slept for a half an hour, washed, then carefully dressed in a blue dimity gown with a smocked bodice. She wished she weren't so flat chested but there was nothing she could do about it. Even her naturally tiny waist wasn't noticeable because of her slim proportions. She took after her mother who stayed as thin as a reed until her death. Oh well, at least she could eat anything and not worry about gaining weight. She must learn to look for the good in everything, she reminded herself.

The dinner, featuring eight courses, began at three o'clock and lasted until five. Mandy was seated next to Smith and across from Tiffany. She could hardly take her eyes off the birthday girl, who chatted about the rice crop as if she were growing it herself. She was just as at ease discussing the bloodlines of the cattle and horses or the many plants in her gardens. She had a natural enthusiasm for all things living and seemed totally unaffected by the family's immense wealth.

Following the dinner, the men retired to the library while Tiffany, Mandy, Miss Thompson, and several of Tiffany's friends walked through the mazes. The pungent smell of the boxwood and the cool air so invigorated Mandy she wanted to run barefoot in and out of the mysterious shapes and dangle her feet in the reflection pool. She felt sure Tiffany would have joined her if the other women had not been present.

Mrs. LaFarge had asked all the guests to reassemble at eight thirty for cake and coffee since there had been so many courses at dinner no one had room for dessert. This was to be Tiffany's surprise party. Mandy wore the ivory satin gown Clarissa had worn to the New Year's Ball. It was a bit too yellow for her complexion but the gown was pure elegance and very flattering for her figure.

When everyone had gathered in the parlor Mr. LaFarge announced they were to go up to the ballroom. There, a full orchestra was playing softly, and on the table a large four tiered birthday cake and gigantic punch bowl awaited the guests. The biggest surprise of all was the appearance of John Clemens, Tiffany's beau, who had been in Rhode Island overseeing the building of a new summer house for the LaFarge family. As the orchestra struck up a waltz, he claimed his astonished sweetheart and whirled her around the floor. After that, several toasts were proposed, then Tiffany opened her gifts. As she prepared to cut her cake, John told her to first open one of the sugar flowers resting on the top tier. As she did, she gasped with surprise, pulling out a ring with a large square cut diamond. Then and there, on bended knee, John officially proposed. For a few minutes bedlam reigned as everyone clapped, laughed, and offered congratulations. Finally the guests settled down to eating and dancing.

"We could have made it a double engagement," whispered Smith into Mandy's ear, as he swirled her around the dance floor.

"Never. I would not want to share a moment that important with anyone. It's too special. Did you see Tiffany's face? She seems to be very much in love with John."

"She should be. He is the son of a neighboring planter and has been courting her since she was sixteen. She will make an excellent plantation wife as she has such an enthusiasm for life, not to mention her expertise with plants and animals."

It was after midnight when Mandy stumbled into bed and fell into a deep sleep. For the first time in months her childhood dream returned. She now recognized the house in her dream as the one on Glebe Street, but to whom was she calling and waving? Sighing in her sleep she began to snore gently until the budgie's chirping awakened her the next morning. She stretched lazily, enjoying the feel of the silk sheets against her body, hoping she could lie in bed a while, as they were not leaving until noon. Then a gentle footstep and a rattle of dishes announced the appearance of a maid with a breakfast tray. Mandy moaned at the interruption. Even the guesthouse had a schedule, and she was expected to conform to its lifestyle. She called to the maid to enter and reached for her robe.

Chapter Twenty

Babs and Mrs. Davies completed the lessons Mandy had prepared for them and had settled into Charleston's society with ease. Now they were needed full time at the hotel because the social season was beginning. Their schooling was over, at least until next summer. Babs had proved to be such an excellent scholar, Miss Thompson was hoping to enroll her in a secondary school, at least part-time.

"I wish I had your wisdom and boldness," said Mandy as Babs, on one of her weekly visits, told Mandy about praying with a distraught woman at the hotel. "The sparks seem to fly right out of your eyes when you talk about Jesus."

"That's the anointing of the Holy Spirit. It's for all Christians and is often called the second blessing or sanctification. It turned John Wesley from a religious weakling into a spiritual giant. Just ask Jesus to baptize you in the Holy Spirit. Why not do it now."

Mandy closed her eyes and uttered a short prayer. She had barely finished when she felt as if she was being bathed in warm oil. Suddenly laughter from deep within bubbled out of her mouth like an artesian well. She had the sensation of total well-being as she continued to laugh until her sides hurt.

Babs clapped her hands in approval. "Aye, the Holy
Spirit's blessing is upon ye, for sure. Thank you, Jesus! As
the Scriptures say, 'The joy of the Lord is my strength.' "

Finally, Mandy's laughter subsided, leaving her breathless. "Goodness! I've never laughed like that before. Where
did all that joy come from? Oh, I feel so clean and light!
Hold me down, so I don't float clear up to heaven. Why
haven't I heard of this before? It's so wonderful!"

"My gram was the one who told Mum about the Holy
Spirit. She had been to one of John Wesley's outdoor
meetings, where the Holy Spirit moved among the people
in a mighty way. People were trembling, laughing, shout-
ing, and praising God. 'Tis the power to share the Gospel
effectively. You'll be bolder in your faith now because
Jesus will seem more real to you."

Babs was right. Mandy couldn't stop reading Scripture. The Bible became so alive she felt as if she was
participating in the very stories themselves. She found
herself singing hymns of praise as she went about her
duties and praying over even the smallest incidences.

With Smith having returned to Pendleton and her
major teaching responsibilities over, her life took on a
slower pace. Of course David Lee came calling once or
twice a week, but Mandy found herself becoming restless.
Helping her cousin grade papers or copy lesson plans just
wasn't enough to keep her occupied.

One morning during breakfast Miss Thompson said,
"Mandy, St. Phillips asked if you would be interested in
a special project. As you know some of the families living
in their debtors' house have children, who are not attending school because of learning disabilities of one sort or
another. They need special tutoring. Would you consider
working with them? You would have to consider it charity
work, as the families would not be able to pay you. You
could meet with the children several afternoons a week

after your regular students have gone. I'm afraid it may interfere with David Lee's visits, but perhaps you two can make other arrangements. I need not remind you this type of tutoring requires creativity and patience. Think about it carefully before you make a decision. It would not be wise to change your mind after you have begun, because these children are often very sensitive to rejection."

Mandy had seen some of the children Miss Thompson was referring to, when she took tea with Babs at the parish house. They would be a handful since their attention span was so short. Still, they were God's creation and deserved to be treated with love and respect. She remembered Susie and Sally Synne. She had taught them many lessons on living by having them actually participate in cooking, sewing, gardening, etc. Perhaps the same type of hands-on program could be used with these children. If they could learn a trade, they could live a useful life that would add to their self- respect. "I'll pray about it, Cousin Caroline. I would certainly need God's help and His blessing. I think I will visit there tomorrow to acquaint myself with the educational needs. I don't want to get in over my head."

Miss Thompson nodded her approval. "Perhaps there is a young mother who would be willing to help you. I suggest you work with no more than three or four at a time. Otherwise you will be doing more baby-sitting than teaching."

The next day at four o'clock Mandy entered the parish house. She could hear children's voices but did not see them until she walked to the back door. A small play area behind the building contained rope swings and a joggling board. Here children were running, tussling, or otherwise playing. She watched them from the back door window. Soon she had mentally placed them into three categories—the bold, the timid, and the curious. She shuttered as she watched an older boy deliberately push a smaller child into the dirt. Then the same boy swaggered over to a chubby girl about eight, who was trying to make a chain out of some flowering weeds. He grabbed the weeds from her hands, threw them to the ground, and began stomping on them. In her rage the girl came at him with fists flying. She managed to land several blows before he pushed her down and began kicking her.

Mandy rushed out the door and down the steps. "Stop it, this instant! Where are your manners? Boys should never hit girls!" She grabbed the bully by the shoulder and held him tightly as he squirmed to get free. "What is your name?"

"LaVerne Cox. Let go of me. I've got as much right to play here as the others. I live here."

"Young man, you were not playing; you were spoiling for a fight. Apologize to that girl, right now!" Still holding his shoulder she pushed him in front of the girl, who was staring open-mouthed at Mandy.

"Sorry," he muttered, scuffling his feet.

"Now go over there to the corner of the fence and pick some more of those flowering weeds. Get long stems so she can make another flower chain." Mandy released him but walked with him to the fence. "Do you know the name of these flowers?" she asked.

"No. Who cares!"

"This is wild marigold. The Indians dried the leaves and used it to keep bugs out of their ground corn and dried berries."

"How do you know? You're no Indian." LaVerne challenged.

"True, but I had a very special Indian friend, named Soaring Hawk, who showed me many of his customs. He helped me when I was running away."

"Running away? You ran away? Who was with you? Where did you go?" Now the boy's anger was forgotten in anticipation of an exciting story.

"I left my home in Tennessee and came to South Carolina in search of my cousin." Mandy sat on the joggling board while the children crowded around her to listen. With wide eyes they followed her adventure. By the end of the tale they considered her a fellow sojourner, whose outcome offered hope to their own homeless plight. Her story finished, Mandy rose to leave, but was stopped by a touch on her arm. With a timid smile the little girl who had been making the flower chain handed it to her. "How beautiful! What a good job you did." Mandy placed it carefully on her head. "What is your name?"

"Katie, miss."

"Why are you not in school, Katie?"

"It's me eyes, miss. They don't see right. I kanna read the letters. I tried, truly I did! But everybody laughed at me; then the teacher sent me home." The earnest look on her face left no doubt she was telling the truth.

"Well, Katie, perhaps I'll have a go at teaching you. Would you be willing to try again?"

"What about me?" growled LaVerne, pushing his way to Mandy's side. "I was here first!"

"Why are you living here?"

"My pa's horse reared up and fell on him. He died two days later. After ma paid our debts, there was nothing left so she sold the house. That's my brother and sister over there, and I've got two more sisters in school." He pointed to several toddlers playing in the dirt. "I hate school. My pa was going to teach me to be a carpenter, like hisself."

"You have to know numbers to be a carpenter. Do you know the difference between feet and yards?"

"Of course. I went to school until this year. I just don't like it. School is for sissies. Look how strong I am. I can work like a man now. I don't need more schoolin'. I need to work to help out my ma." He bent his arm showing Mandy his muscle.

Mandy sensed the fear in LaVerne. His father was dead, making him the man of the family, yet he was unsure of his ability to function as an adult. He was acting the part of the bully not because of excess self-esteem but from a lack of it. Mandy searched for something positive to say. "You seem strong enough, LaVerne. It's thoughtful and considerate of you to want to help your mother support the family. I'm sure the right opportunity will soon come your way." She made a mental note to ask David if his father would consider taking on the boy at the shipyards.

One by one the children introduced themselves and told their stories of hard times, deaths in the family, or ruthless landlords. By the time Mandy left she was overwhelmed by their seemingly hopeless situations. How could she help? She wondered if the members of St. Phillips knew how desperate some of these families really were. If the children were struggling so, what must it be like for the adults? She decided to return another time and talk with some of the mothers.

"My heart ached listening to the sad tales the children told," she told Miss Thompson that evening. "Most of them are certainly capable of learning something. I suspect part of the problem is that, due to their destitute situation, the teachers don't want to be bothered with them. If they are disruptive in class it is because they need some recognition; they are looking for someone to care."

"Enough of the problem," said Miss Thompson, dryly. "What solutions do you have to offer?"

"I'm not sure. I was hoping you might find work for some of the women, paid employment. Perhaps someone could teach them a skill like sewing or the millinery craft. I wish the elders of the church would assume more responsibility."

"I'll talk to them and their wives, if you will agree to head a committee on behalf of the children. We need young blood in that department."

"All right. There are about six that have special educational needs. The smallest children just need more careful supervision. LaVerne and the other older boys and girls should be taught trades. Just because they aren't college material doesn't mean they are any less gifted or important."

"I like your enthusiasm. See if you can talk your friend David into getting involved. The boys need a man to work with them. Money does have influence, and he has many contacts through his family."

When David called for Mandy on Saturday to take her to the theater, she regaled him with her ideas to help the people at St. Phillips.

"You are such a good teacher, David. Your reputation is impeccable. What a wonderful mentor you would be for the older boys. Can I count on your assistance? Perhaps we could find two other teachers and form a committee. When work is divided it does not seem nearly as overwhelming. It would be an opportunity for us to work together."

David gave Mandy an indulgent smile. "So, my barefoot sea urchin has become a fairy godmother. I would like to help, but my free time is almost nonexistent now that school is in session. I will come to your first meeting after you find other willing teachers. In the meantime, I will think of creative ways to teach your waifs. Mother will have a fit if I am not around to escort her to her meetings and teas. Father means well, but even when he is home he is usually immersed in business of some sort. I will ask him to hire one or two of the oldest, strongest boys as shipbuilder apprentices because I believe everyone, boy or girl, should have at least one employable trade as insurance against the poor house."

David helped Mandy from the carriage. He hoped she wasn't so preoccupied with her project that she would not enjoy the play, as the tickets had cost him a large part of his weekly salary. A Shakespearean troupe from London was offering a series of the playwright's works. Tonight the program was *MacBeth*.

By the end of the first act, Mandy was totally absorbed in the story. She shuttered at the tyranny and clenched her fists during the scenes of intrigue. When the final curtain fell she was emotionally spent.

"David! That was wonderful! Gruesome, but wonderful. The acting was superb. I felt as if I were a mouse in the corner of the castle."

On the way home David let the horse amble. He tucked Mandy's arm in his and drew her close. "I would like to make your birthday special, but I'm afraid I will be gone all weekend. One of the platoons at The Citadel is going on maneuvers, and I am to accompany them. We are leaving Thursday evening and won't return until late Sunday. I'm sorry to neglect you, but maybe this will help ease the pain." Reaching into his waistcoat pocket he produced a small box wrapped in a piece of red silk. Mandy unwrapped it carefully. Inside the box was a gold ring containing a small diamond surrounded by tiny rubies.

"It's beautiful!"

"It belonged to my grandmother Hattie. She was very fond of rings and wore one on almost every finger. I would like you to consider it a special friendship ring. Wear it everyday and think of me." David said with devotion in his voice.

Mandy slipped the ring on the little finger of her right hand. It fit perfectly. She was glad it was a friendship ring and nothing more serious. "Thank you, David. You have made my birthday memorable. I truly think of you as a special friend and rely on you more than you know. I will wear this ring with pride." They rode along in silence as Mandy thought about David. Did her future lie with this energetic young man whose family was well known in Charleston society? Could she become a socialite, with its political and social demands? Was this God's will? She doubted her ability to adapt to the posturing elite and supposed she would only hold David back from whatever ladders of success he desired to climb. Would the real Mandy please make herself known, she fervently prayed.

Chapter Twenty-One

Mandy stomped into the house, closing the door with a bang. What was the matter with people? Why was it so hard to find teachers willing to help the children of St. Phillips? She had spent the whole week looking for support for her project, but to no avail. Meanwhile, the children waited.

Miss Thompson had talked to the church elders, but had not received much encouragement except for Mr. Whitfield, a retired teacher, who offered his services two afternoons a week. Mandy had wanted a younger person, but decided to take whatever help was available. She notified David of a planning meeting and was disappointed when he sent a portfolio of lesson plans but did not come in person. As it turned out, Miss Thompson added her presence, making it a threesome. They decided to reinstate all possible children into the school system, notifying the teachers that the slower children would be tutored in difficult subjects. That left five students, who needed personal instruction because of physical problems—Katie, who was dyslectic; John, whose high fever as a baby had left him hard of hearing; Neal, a nervous boy of seven, who could not concentrate; and Jennifer and Mark, twins, both slow learners. It was agreed Mandy would teach the class, while Mr. Whitfield gave individual instruction, then they would reverse roles. Miss Thompson suggested they teach by rote as much as possible, devoting an hour each day to hands-on projects to keep the children interested. She shook her head at the thought of dealing with such a variety of challenges.

Mr. Whitfield proved to be the perfect teacher. He was strict and orderly, but had a wonderful sense of humor, often breaking the tension with a joke or antic which made the children dissolve into giggles. His favorite trick was wearing a special hat and becoming the character the hat symbolized. The children learned of George Washington, Gallileo, Alexander the Great, and other historic personages, as Mr. Whitfield acted out their biographies. Soon he was coming every day to help and referring to the children as "my students."

David had devised a test to be given to the older children who wanted to leave school in order to learn a trade. It was a general knowledge exam, heavy on practical information that Mandy found useful in preparing her lesson plans. She was, after all, working with children who needed the basics. Two afternoons a week the girls and boys separated for special classes, where a seamstress taught the girls and a carpenter, the boys. For most it was their favorite time. John showed a natural aptitude for woodworking, caressing the wood in his hands and taking pains that all pieces fit exactly. Here was something he could learn by watching instead of through listening. He quickly grasped how to cut angles and corners, beaming with pride when the carpenter praised his work.

Katie spent hours copying the alphabet properly, but it was slow going. Mandy made flash cards of simple words and numbers to help her reading, but more than once Katie dissolved into tears of frustration. "Its no use! I'll never learn. I just don't see like other people. Why did God make me like this? I hate myself! I wish I was dead!"

"Hush, Katie! Don't say such things!" Mandy gathered the weeping girl into her arms. "God made you special, and He never makes a mistake. You may not be able to read well, but you are a natural mother. I've seen you help the twins many times, and I know you look after the toddlers at St. Phillips. You have a heart that delights in helping others which is a wonderful gift. The way you make flower chains shows you are very skillful in using your hands. Look at your lovely fingers, so long and slender. Those are the fingers of an artist." Mandy continued pointing out Katie's' attributes until she felt the little girl relax. Then she sent her to the garden to pick flowers for an arrangement. It took a half-hour of concentration before Katie called the project finished. The arrangement was beautifully done and included sprigs of boxwood and ivy for greenery. Mandy lavishly praised her work. Katie smiled happily, her momentary despair forgotten.

Neal was the biggest problem. He would not sit still, making teaching him almost impossible. He wandered around the room or sat in his chair rocking back and forth. He would answer a question correctly, showing he was listening, but he could not focus enough to read or write. Then one day during recess a puppy wandered into the yard. Neal rushed over and picked him up, receiving a thorough face washing from the puppy's tongue.

"May I keep him, Miss Greene? He is so thin, he must be a stray. He needs a bath, too. Please let me keep him here. I'm not allowed a dog at the parish house."

Mandy had a brilliant idea. "You may keep him if he does not belong to anyone, but you will have to train and care for him. If you forget, I will give the puppy to someone who will be more responsible."

"I'll brush and feed him everyday, I promise. I'm going to call him Marco Polo because he wandered from home. Here, Marco; come, boy." The puppy, which had wriggled out of Neal's grasp to inspect a palmetto bug, obligingly trotted over, his scraggly tail wagging furiously.

"Phew! He smells awful! I'll get some soap. Use that bucket by the rain barrel and scrub every inch of him. Be sure to rinse him well, and don't get any soap in his eyes or ears." Mandy hurried off to get the soap before Neal lost interest. To her surprise he was still in the same place when she returned. "Here is a short piece of rope to tie him with because some dogs don't like water."

Neal tied the rope around the puppy's neck then led him to the rain barrel. Soon both dog and boy were covered with soapy water. Amazingly, Neal stuck with his task until the puppy was rinsed and toweled dry. It was the first time Mandy had seen him finish a project. She praised him profusely and added an extra ten minutes of play time to his recess, so he could walk his new friend until they both were dry. The puppy proved to be the key to Neal's education. After completing a lesson, he was rewarded with time to train and play with his dog, an activity enthusiastically shared by both.

The second Friday in November found Mandy feverishly packing a small trunk in preparation for the weekend with the Gibbes. She was anxious to see them, hear their stories, and share her own. The relaxed atmosphere of the plantation appealed to her and, although she hated to admit it, having a servant attend to her for a day or two seemed the height of luxury.

Soon, Jacob was knocking on the door, the buggy ready to carry her to the Beaufort countryside. To Mandy's delight, Mrs. Gibbes had come to Charleston to shop so the time on the road passed quickly.

"You will find the girls more mature. Europe was just the adventure they needed to broaden their horizons. The diversity of people and customs has taught them to be more tolerant and accepting. However, I don't see why

Annabelle is so infatuated with Paris. I found the people to be quite bohemian and uncultured. Seemingly, they have few morals and even less hygiene. The smells on the streets were sickening. It's no wonder they douse themselves with perfume." Mrs. Gibbes waved a fan in front on her face, as she recalled the offending odors.

Mandy smiled to herself as she remembered the odor she had had to endure while hiding under the chicken coop. It seemed like another world to her now.

Mrs. Gibbes continued her recount of Europe then suddenly stopped in mid sentence. "Jacob! Jacob! What's the matter?" She half rose from her seat, clutching the side of the carriage to prevent falling. Mandy, sitting with her back to the elderly driver, turned around to see what was happening as the surrey began to pick up speed. She saw Jacob slumped along the seat, the reins slack in a lifeless hand. The horses, which been trotting at a collected pace were now moving rapidly, feeling no resistance on their bits.

"Mandy, do something! Stop the horses! O God, help us! Help us!" shrieked Mrs. Gibbes, desperately holding on to the side of the bouncing surrey with one hand and her large rose covered straw hat with the other. It was evident the surrey would soon topple over if the horses, now in a full gallop, were not soon brought under control. Mandy bent over the back of the seat and tried to reach the reins, but Jacob's arm was between the seat and the floor. Hoisting her dress above her knees to give her more freedom, she leaned as far over the driver's seat as possible, but the reins were still three inches out of reach. By now the surrey was swaying wildly from side to side as the horses, panic stricken from the slapping traces, began to weave across the road, their manes and tails streaming behind them, and their nostrils flaring with each breath.

Steadying herself as best she could, Mandy belly slid

over the back of the driver's seat, almost knocking Jacob's
body off the carriage. She fell head first onto the floor,
grabbing the reins as she slid past. With her feet braced
against the wooden footboard she began sawing on the
reins, pulling back as hard as she could. "Whoa! Whoa!"
she yelled at the top of her voice. The horses seemed
almost relieved at finding a human in control again, and
gradually came to a stop, their sides heaving and frothy
foam covering their bodies where the harness leather
touched them.

"Are you all right, Mrs. Gibbes?" Mandy was afraid to
take her eyes off the nervous beasts, lest they begin running again.

"I think so, let me catch my breath. Goodness, what
a wild ride. I guess there's no serious damage done. Is
Jacob dead or alive?"

"I think he's passed, ma'am. I don't see him breathing,
and his eyes are wide open."

"Poor soul. Well, he died doing his duty. I hope the
good Lord takes that into account. Jacob was as faithful
as the day is long. I shall miss him. Can you handle those
animals? If so, I think we should continue on, at a slower
pace, of course." Mrs. Gibbes burst into hysterical laughter at her little joke, releasing the inner terror of the last
few minutes.

Mandy laughed, too. The woman had mettle, to be
sure. She straightened herself out so she could sit on the
driver's seat, clucked to the horses, relaxed the reins, and
off they went. Two hours later, the familiar pillars denot-
ing the road to the Gibbes' plantation came into view.
Mandy breathed a sigh of relief, knowing she would soon
be standing on solid ground.

As they stopped at the front entrance, several of the
yard workers, having seen Jacob's crumpled body and
Mandy in the driver's seat, rushed to help. Removing

Jacob from the carriage, they carried him to his cabin where his wife and daughter began wailing in grief.

"There will be no sleeping tonight," Mrs. Gibbes said sadly, as she climbed from the surrey. "These people seem determined to usher their own into the pearly gates on wings of song, if you can call that caterwauling song. No doubt they'll build a roaring fire, then weep and wail until daybreak. Come, Mandy, we need a cup of strong tea to revive our spirits. Annabelle! Clarissa! Mandy is here. Come greet your guest!"

With a servant holding the horses, Mandy retrieved her trunk and half carried, half dragged it up the steps and into the front hall. News of Jacob's untimely death had already reached the ears of the other household servants, and they had gone to console his family.

"Mama, are you all right? What has happened? Mandy, did you drive those nasty horses? I thought only papa and Jacob could handle that pair." Clarissa hugged her mother then kissed Mandy on both cheeks, French style. Mandy smiled but made no effort to return her kisses.

"Clarissa, we need a cup of tea, now. Be a dear and see to it. Where's Annabelle? Mandy, make yourself comfortable. Your old room is ready for you. Leave the trunk right there, I'll have someone take it up later. I must wash the road dirt off my face." Mrs. Gibbes hurried to her room, leaving Mandy still standing in the hall. Unsure of what to do, she followed Clarissa to the outdoor kitchen where she could rinse off and get something to eat. Now that the excitement was over she discovered she was starving.

The next day was declared Mandy's special day by virtue of her belated birthday, so she had breakfast in bed accompanied by Clarissa and Annabelle who wore her out describing their experiences in Europe. Clarissa produced a silhouette of her beau that Annabelle had drawn. Mandy voiced the expected approval and admiration. It was evident Clarissa was hoping to be wearing an engagement ring by Christmas. Annabelle displayed a portfolio of drawings done while attending art classes in Paris. Some seemed reasonably good to Mandy who confessed she knew next to nothing about art. By the time the girls wound down, Mandy was so tired of the incessant chatter that she decided to reserve her tales until dinner.

At three o'clock, dressed in her blue dimity, she entered the dining room. The long cherry table sparkled with silver and crystal, Mrs. Gibbes' way of showing her appreciation of Mandy's bravery. As one course followed another she told the family about the Welsh newcomers, her acceptance of Jesus, and the young children at the parish house.

"Perhaps special glasses may help the girl with the reading problems," stated Dr. Gibbes, thoughtfully. "I will give you the name of an eye specialist in Charleston, who will check little Katie free of charge. Hopefully her sight can be improved. I'm afraid there is not much help for the deaf boy. Teaching him to identify words so he can read is about the best you can do, since he is already able to read lips. I'd concentrate on a vocation for him, especially since he seems interested in carpentry. Skilled carpenters are in great demand and command a goodly wage."

As they were talking, a servant entered carrying a large double layer cake covered with glowing candles. "Happy Birthday, Mandy! Many more!" The genuine affection from the Gibbes made Mandy a bit teary-eyed. How blest she was to have them as an extended family. She blew out the candles, cut the cake, and pronounced it delicious.

"It's a recipe we got in Italy. It's made with oranges and coconut," said Clarissa. "We sat outside at a little cafe overlooking the sea the first time we tasted it. Hurry and finish eating, Mandy. We want to give you your presents."

Annabelle set a stack of brightly wrapped packages in front of Mandy. All the gifts had come from Europe—art books from Paris, lace from Vienna, a tartan from Scotland, and a small marble statue from Italy. She was overwhelmed by their thoughtfulness.

After the party was over the three girls went for a walk. "Mandy, you seemed so much more settled. The determined look you always wore on your face has been replaced by a serene glow making you seem more approachable. Is it because you have found your family or because of your beaus?" asked Clarissa.

"Both. I have joined my true family, the family of God and my dearest beau is Jesus Christ. I love Him with all my heart. I never knew Christianity contained so much peace and joy, besides the adventure of following God's will every day."

"I thought you became a Christian when you started going to church. I think I've always been a Christian, I was baptized as a baby and have been in church all my life," commented Annabelle as she picked a late-blooming daisy and tucked it behind one ear.

"People have different experiences and beliefs, but I think when Jesus told Nicodemus he had to be born again, He meant we had to personally ask Jesus to forgive our sins and then accept by faith His transforming grace in our lives. There is a scripture that says through Jesus we are taken out of the kingdom of darkness—meaning the devil's realm—and placed into the kingdom of light—God's kingdom. I believe a definite act of repentance is required before you can be received by God. Otherwise everyone who goes to church could call themselves Christians, and we all know some attend church out of duty while others go because it's good for their businesses. When I was living with you I went because it was expected of me, and even though I prayed sometimes and thought about God,

I was still an unbeliever. But not anymore! I can truly say Jesus is my loving friend and guide. It's wonderful!"

"I can see that it is," replied Clarissa. "I wish I had your assurance of spiritual things. I will think on what you said."

"Mandy! Stop! Don't take another step," hissed Annabelle. Mandy froze and looked down. A few feet away a snake lay semi-coiled, its white, membranous mouth open in warning. "It's a cottonmouth. They're poisonous. Papa said if I ever came upon one to stand still for a few minutes then back away very slowly. Don't take your eyes off it. Try to stare it down."

The girls stood immovable for what seemed an eternity, staring into the black, bottomless depths of the snake's glittering eyes. Its tongue flashed like forked lightening, while the head swayed gently from side to side. Finally, the snake decided it was no longer being threatened and slithered away into the reeds.

"He's gone, thank goodness! Let's go back. I remember reading a Scripture that says if a snake bites a believer they won't be harmed, but I am not ready to put that verse to the test!" Mandy turned and quickly began to walk toward the house. The sunset cast a golden glow over the sky, making the river seem like molten metal. Even the house took on an ethereal glow.

"How beautiful! Perhaps this is a little piece of heaven on earth, and we are walking the streets of gold," mused Annabelle, wishing she could freeze the scene until she could get it on canvas.

"I'll be very disappointed if heaven is like this. It's supposed to be a place of peace and joy. Here there is so much talk of secession, I doubt we will enjoy peace much longer," remarked Clarissa, prophetically.

"Yes, Smith said some of the men in Pendleton were stockpiling weapons. War is terrible. It scares me just to

think about it. What will happen? How will we manage
if all the men are off fighting?" replied Mandy.

"Let's talk of more pleasant things. This is your birthday and it should be a happy time. Race you to the house."
Annabelle began to run like a bird in flight—her curls
bobbing, one hand holding up her dress, the other out-
stretched. Mandy and Clarissa, laughing and breathless,
soon overtook her and the trio, sounding like a herd of
elephants, bounded up the back steps.

The following afternoon Mandy waved good-bye to
her surrogate family, not knowing it was the last time she
would see them all together.

Chapter Twenty-Two

It began the first day of December in the evening fog. A ship loaded with Asian imports docked in the Charleston harbor after weeks at sea. The sailors, anxious for solid ground and companionship, scattered in every direction including one lad who had a low-grade fever and felt "off his feed." That night he kissed a flirtatious barmaid, infecting her. She passed it along to her customers and soon a fierce influenza epidemic was spreading rampantly through Charleston. Residents were warned to stay inside their houses or leave the city. Because Christmas and the peak of the social season was days away, people were loathed to make an escape, afraid of missing the holiday gaiety.

Miss Thompson treated the whole situation with disdain. "I've lived through hurricanes, fires, and yellow fever, whatever minor interruption this causes me is not worth the worry. I will continue my tutoring for another week as scheduled."

Mandy followed suit. She was working with two young women, besides the children at the parish house, who were progressing by leaps and bounds. They were her special joy and a deep bond was growing between her and her "gifted students," as she called them.

By the week's end the weather had turned cold and wet. Rain fell steadily, reinforced by a sharp wind off the ocean that drove the bone-chilling damp into every nook and cranny. Miss Thompson kept the fires in the parlor and bedrooms burning constantly.

Saturday, a letter arrived from Smith saying he had decided to stay in Pendleton, as he was in the process of purchasing an adjoining farm owned by a young widow of exceptional charm and beauty. He apologized for not writing sooner and wished her a happy Christmas.

Mandy read between the lines. Smith was ready for marriage and the opportunity had no doubt presented itself. Had she been wrong to put him off? She thought of the passion his presence kindled within her. Just the reaction of a teen's raging hormones, she concluded, since she felt no great desire to resign herself to plantation life in Pendleton. Surely there was more to love than tingly feelings. There had to be a meeting of the minds, a desire to commit one's whole identity to another person. She had not felt that way toward Smith, nor did David provoke her deepest affection. There was a part of her she was reluctant to share with anyone. Perhaps she just needed more time to mature. Whatever the reason, she mourned the loss of Smith's affections for several hours then put all the "what ifs" out of her mind. She had given her life to Christ, let Him handle the details. She felt guilty not being more upset, but there were other situations of greater importance to deal with at the present. She made a cup of tea and returned to her studies.

The Monday of Christmas recess Mandy noticed her cousin wearing a heavy shawl and coughing repeatedly when she tried to talk. A home remedy of whiskey and honey seemed to quell the coughing for a while, but when it returned it was worse than before.

"Shall I send for Dr. McGee?" asked Mandy, after her cousin struggled through a particularly long coughing spell.

"He is too busy with flu victims to be bothered with my small problems," gasped Miss Thompson. "I'm sure I'll be better tomorrow."

But when tomorrow came, Mandy found her in bed with a raging fever and surrounded with soiled bedclothes. "Stay away from me. Send for Trudy from St. Phillips. She'll know what to do. I don't want you exposed to this sickness," moaned Cousin Caroline.

"I've already been exposed," replied Mandy, calmly. "And I know what to do. You are my only family, and I believe in taking care of my kin." She replaced the bedding and filled a basin with cool water with which to bathe her cousin's fever-ridden form. All day and far into the night she sat beside the bed forcing liquids down a spastic throat and sponging the overheated body. She had sent for Dr. McGee but was told he would come when he could, as he was busy writing the death certificates of the victims of the epidemic.

Above Miss Thompson's raspy breathing and coughing episodes, Mandy could hear the rattle of the death wagons with their load of human remains passing on the street below. A thousand prayers crossed her lips as she ministered to her cousin and thought of the families who had lost loved ones. She fingered the little silver cross hanging around her neck. How precious it seemed to her now that she understood its significance. Could it be her mother had given it to her hoping one day she would find its meaning?

"Thank you, ma, for this special gift. I'll never be alone again, no matter what happens to Cousin Caroline. I am part of God's family, now. I know Jesus is alive and has sent His angels to watch over me. Oh, how blest I am!"

By the time Dr. McGee arrived the following day, Miss Thompson was delirious with fever and struggling to breathe. "Her lungs are full of fluid," he said. "I'll leave some medicine to keep her as comfortable as possible. Try to get it down her. It's only a matter of time, now." He placed a bottle into Mandy's shaking hand. "Get some sleep, girl, or you'll be next," he advised as he walked out the door.

After several spoonfuls of medicine her cousin seemed to rest more quietly, so Mandy lay down on the chaise in the adjoining room. She meant only to rest, but sleep overtook her, and for hours she was oblivious to sight or sound. When she awoke it was dark; the fires had reduced themselves to embers, and she was uncomfortably cold. Hastily adding more wood to the coals, she went to check on her cousin.

Miss Thompson was awake; her bright, feverish eyes fastened on Mandy. "I'm on my way to meet my Maker," she wheezed. "You've been like a daughter to me. I'm so glad we found each other. Mr. Simons, my attorney, has my will. Don't settle for second best, Mandy. Set your sights high." From out of the covers came a trembling hand, which Mandy held gently.

"Oh, Cousin Caroline, what will I do without you? You have taught me so much. You are my very best friend. I love you with all my heart!" Tears streamed down her cheeks, as she stroked her cousin's face now in the throes of death. After a quiet sigh, the hand went limp, and a silence so thick it could be felt encompassed the room. Still weeping uncontrollably Mandy pulled the coverlet over her cousin's face, then went to notify the doctor.

Miss Thompson's burial was one of four done simultaneously at St. Phillips. The few mourners in attendance were mostly family members, as the normal populace sought protection from the sickness by staying within the confines of their homes. After the brief service, Mandy lingered, reluctant to say her final good-bye. New graves dotted the cemetery, and the diggers were even there preparing others. She felt numb with grief, unable to think, refusing to believe the awful truth that she was alone again. She dreaded going back to the empty house, so she slowly walked to St. Phillips' parish house to check on her students, as it had been nearly a week since she had seen them. Katie met her at the door.

"Oh, Miss Greene, I'm so glad you're here!" Katie burst into tears, flinging herself into Mandy's arms. "Five people have died, including Neal's mum and the twins. Now my mother is in bed with a fever. I'm so scared! Are we all going to die? Will there be anyone left? I watch the death wagon go up and down the street every day collecting someone. Is God mad at us? Why is He letting this happen?"

Mandy rocked her gently in her arms. "We won't all die, I'm sure of that, but I don't know God's mind in this matter. Go get your cloak and a change of underwear, then tell the house mistress that you will be staying with me for a few days until your mother gets better. I need the company." She gave Katie a hug then pushed her toward the stairway. While she waited for her return, Mandy noticed an embroidered panel hanging on the wall. 'The Lord is my Shepherd, I shall not want,' it read. "Oh, Jesus, shepherd me! I need you now more than ever. You are the only comfort I have." A tear threatened to trickle down her face, but she hurriedly brushed it away. It would not do Katie any good to see her teacher crying.

A few moments later Katie reappeared with Neal in tow. Each was carrying a ragged satchel. "Miss Greene, Neal wants to come, too. He's all alone, and nobody has time to care for him properly. He's been sitting in the dark in his room. It's all right, isn't it? I told Mrs. Pritchard; she didn't seem to mind."

"Of course Neal is welcome. I've plenty of room." She looked at the dirty, disheveled little boy, whose blank expression mirrored the shock of his mother's death. "Your puppy has missed you. He needs your love and care." She put an arm around each child and walked them home.

That evening after a supper of soup and stale bread made palatable by some of Miss Thompson's fig marmalade, Mandy prepared the children for bed by providing a hot, relaxing bath for each. Then she gave them clean shifts to wear as nightshirts. Neal grumbled a bit at having to wear women's clothes, but he was so relieved at having someone tend him his rebellion was short lived. Mandy gave Katie her room then bedded Neal on the horsehair sofa in the parlor. She banked both fires so the rooms would stay warm, gathered some extra quilts for herself and chose the settee in the morning room as her bed. Tomorrow she would clean her cousin's room and move Neal into it.

In the dark of the night Mandy fought her fears of being homeless again. "What will become of us? Lord Jesus, I know you love us. Please find us a house or somewhere to stay. I don't want the children out on the streets or in an orphanage." After a fitful night's sleep she rose early and went to the kitchen to prepare her charges a special breakfast of grits, ham biscuits, and fruit. The large pile of laundry demanded immediate attention, so she began the chore of heating water for the washing tub. The sunrise promised an end to the damp, gray skies, and by midmorning brilliant yellow rays, shining through lacy clouds, were warming the air.

The children were in a festive mood, actually enjoying the endless chores she had planned for the day. Soon clothes and bedding were line drying, while she and Katie washed down the walls and furniture in Miss Thompson's room. Neal vigorously scrubbed the floor with strong lye soap then opened all the windows to air it thoroughly. By dinner time they were exhausted. Mandy fed them the last of the soup and biscuits, some dried apple cobbler, and greens from the garden. When the kitchen had been cleaned, she declared the rest of the day a holiday, allowing the children to do as they pleased. Neal went to play with his puppy; Katie wanted to make herself a proper nightgown. Mandy rummaged through her cousin's clothes until she found a heavy cotton petticoat. Together she and Katie undid all the seams and cut it to fit the little girl. While Katie was stitching it together, Mandy went to check on Neal. To her delight he was cleaning the yard, piling fallen branches in a corner near the house and raking the leaves into piles under the trees.

"That looks wonderful, Neal. The garden has needed cleaning for weeks. If you can break up some of those dead limbs we will use them in the fireplaces." A few minutes later Neal came to the kitchen door with an arm load of wood that he dumped into a large wooden box.

"This calls for a story," said Mandy, reaching for a book of Dickens, while gathering Neal and Katie to her side on the sofa. She read for about fifteen minutes before they were interrupted by a rapid knocking on the front door. Neal ran to open it. "It's Reverend McMurtry from St. Phillips," he announced.

Mandy's heart sank. The news had to be bad. She fixed a smile on her face and invited him into the parlor. The Reverend looked as if he had not slept in days. His hollowed eyes looked at Mandy sadly. "It's Katie's mother. She died an hour ago. We have several others to bury, so we will add her to the list. The service will be tomorrow morning at ten o'clock. As far as we know she had no other relatives in these parts. Will you look after Katie until other arrangements can be made? I'm sorry to burden you, but there are so many ill. . . ."

"I will be happy to keep Katie as long as necessary, and other children, too, if you can find no one else to tend them. I'll tell Katie about her mother. Do you have time for a cup of tea?"

"I'm afraid not. So many need the services of the church at this time. It's amazing how many souls need to confess their sins when facing death. I do what I can. However, Jesus is the only mediator between God and man. He alone holds the keys to heaven and hell, and is the judge of all. I am just His servant and have no special powers. 'Tis frustrating, at times like these."

Mandy nodded sympathetically. Why did people ignore God until on their deathbeds? After wasting their life, how could they expect heavenly rewards? She felt a heaviness in her heart as she walked the reverend to the door then returned to her wards.

"Come sit here by me, Katie. Reverend McMurtry asked me to tell you about your mother. She is with Jesus now in her heavenly home. Her earthly sorrows are ended. She died a little while ago. The funeral is tomorrow."

"Not my ma, ooh, no! My beautiful ma! Why her? She was so good! Ooh, no," Katie's sobs were muffled as she buried her face in Mandy's chest. Neal stood in the doorway, tears streaming down his face, as he remembered seeing his own mother lying white and still in death. He shuffled over and sat at Mandy's feet his face pressed against her skirt which absorbed his tears. For a while Mandy sat silently, allowing the children to vent their grief. When their sobs began to subside into sniffles, she started telling them about the New Jerusalem, their heavenly home.

"Your heavenly city is very beautiful," she said. "It is made of pure gold, the walls are beautiful gems of various colors. There are twelve gates, each made of a single huge pearl, and the streets are pure gold but transparent, like glass. Best of all the glory of Jesus shines so brightly there is no need of sun or moon for light. It is a very wonderful place, filled with love, joy, and everything good, much better than the very best of anything here on earth. Your mothers are very happy there."

"Do you think they can see us?" asked Neal, hopefully.

"I'm not sure, but I know God has angels ready to help and guide us when we need them. Perhaps they are substitute mothers, in a way. You can keep the image of your mother in your heart by always remembering all the good things about her. That's comforting, isn't it?"

Neal nodded. It was nice to have someone understand what he was going through. He reached up and took Katie's hand. "Katie, I'll be your pretend brother and look out for you as much as I can, and Mandy can be our pretend mother. That way we can always be together."

Katie stopped sniffling and gave Neal a watery smile. "That's nice. Then we'll all be part of the same family. I like that."

"So do I," said Mandy, giving each child a hug.

Mr. Simons was the next visitor, coming just as Mandy, Katie, and Neal returned home from the burial services. "Beg pardon, Miss Greene, but I did not want you to expose yourself to the general public lest you take sick, so I took the liberty of preparing the necessary papers advising you of Miss Thompson's will."

"Please come in. The library is the best place for business matters. Katie, please see that we are not disturbed." Mandy ushered Mr. Simons into the cypress paneled room. "Feel free to use the desk. May I offer you some refreshment?"

"No, thank you. This will just take a minute. I told the carriage driver to wait. As you know your cousin was renting this house from St. Phillips church. They advised me that they would be happy to continue to rent it to you at the same fee. I believe this situation must have been arranged by Miss Thompson, as she has provided funds to pay for the rental for the next ten years should you decide to stay here that long. She also left you a monthly living allowance of three hundred dollars."

"Three hundred dollars! That's a fortune!"

"Not hardly, but it is enough to keep body and soul together until your tutoring business is established. You are to have all her personal belongings. Her remaining funds are to go to support St. Phillips parish house, a worthy cause, indeed. Now if you will sign here. . . ."

Mandy could hardly hold the pen steady as she signed the release papers. She was not to be out in the street after all! God had heard her prayers and provided her with room and board for ten whole years.

When Mr. Simons left after giving Mandy her first check, she stood in the hallway clapping her hands for joy. "Thank you, Jesus! You said the righteous would never be forsaken. Thank you! Thank you!"

Katie and Neal watched with surprise. They had never seen anyone talk to God and dance a jig at the same time. Mandy rushed over and gave them a hug. "We won't have to move after all! This lovely house and spacious yard is ours to use for the next ten years. God is so good!"

It was New Year's Eve before the epidemic had run its course, and Charleston returned to some semblance of normalcy. All parties were canceled out of respect for the dead and their families. Almost every household in the city had lost someone. St. Phillips' parish house had been hit especially hard; five adults and four children had died. Mandy found herself taking in Beth, a four year old, now an orphan and within the space of two days, John, six, and Samuel, three, were referred to her. The house rang with childish laughter and tears, often sending her to her knees in prayer for the wisdom to soothe breaking hearts or find diplomatic solutions to territorial disputes.

David Lee appeared on her doorstep the week after New Years, profusely apologetic for not being her main stay during the disaster.

"Mother insisted we all go to the summer house at Folly Beach," he said. "Once there she decided to stay until after Christmas. What could I do? I'm her only son. I was kept busy searching for driftwood to keep the bitter ocean gales from making the house too cold to inhabit. Are you folks all right?"

"Cousin Caroline died of pneumonia. I haven't gotten over the shock of it, yet. Thanks to God she left me the means to stay here for ten years, and with it came a new family," Mandy said, smiling at the youngsters clustered around her who were staring at David. David stared back incredulously.

"You are minding five children? Have they no families? Do you plan to keep them? How will you care for them all? Aren't there local orphanages that will take them?"

"Cousin Caroline left me some money for living expenses. We will manage as we trust the Lord to provide. David, I truly believe this is what the Lord wants of me in this hour. I understand the need for love and security these little ones have. It wasn't so long ago I was in the same straits. Had I not been taken in by the Gibbes, heaven only knows where I'd be." She stood straight and tall, radiating her faith. David, on the other hand, seemed to shrink before her eyes.

"Well, this is a great undertaking for one so young. I wish I could help, but my teaching responsibilities are so heavy just now that I'm not sure when I will be able to call on you again. The school is scheduling more field exercises, and I must accompany the cadets on most of them.

I wish you the best of luck. Feel free to call on me whenever necessary." David shuffled backward toward the door,
a sheepish look on his face.

Mandy realized he was unable to face the prospect of
so much responsibility and was saying his good-byes. She
smiled at him gently. How fickle and fearful men were
when confronted with situations not of their own doing.
One minute he was pledging his love; now he was backing
away. She could not blame him; this was her calling, not
his. God evidently did not plan for David to share her
situation.

"I understand, David, truly I do. I will be happy to see
you whenever you wish to visit. I wish you God's bless-
ings in whatever life holds for you." She accompanied him
to the door, closing it gently behind him. Again the decision had been made for her; she was not to become Mrs.
David Lee.

That night after the children were tucked in bed and
had said their prayers, Mandy drew a parlor chair close to
the dwindling fire and stared into the glowing embers.
Had she made the right decision choosing the children
over David? There was a certain amount of stability in
marriage, especially when the man came from a wealthy
family. Yet David had retreated quickly when confronted
by the children. Would he be just as prone to run from
family responsibilities after marriage? Perhaps Cousin
Caroline had left her the inheritance so she could take her
time choosing a mate and not have to rush into a commitment for convenience's sake. Yet, who could read another's
heart? There was no guarantee any marriage would be
fulfilling or last a lifetime. She sighed and added more
wood to the fire, causing the flames to flare upward suddenly. Some lives were like that, she thought, burning
brightly for a short time then turning to cold ashes. That
was not the lifestyle she wanted; defeat was not a word in

her vocabulary. She planned to be useful until she drew her last breath, her steps following the footprints of her Savior. Nor did she want to live as Miss Ellie or Mrs. Fortune, whose bitterness and resentment of their life situations spilled over to everyone they met. Although professing to be Christians they worshipped a religion of their own making rather than the person of Jesus Christ. True Christianity meant showing the same mercy and love to others as Christ had shown to her.

Once in bed, in the midst of deep slumber, her dream returned. Again she stood at the gate of the large brick house waving and calling as usual, when suddenly the scene enlarged to reveal children, large and small, coming down a dusty road. Overhead a winged angel with out-stretched arms seemed to be gently guiding them to Mandy, who was calling out words of encouragement and welcome. Mandy woke with a start, the dream clearly etched in her mind. At last she understood. God was calling her to a special task—a ministry to children. She had been right in accepting the little ones. "Thank you, Lord Jesus," she whispered into the darkness. "You have been with me all the way and have turned the bitter times into sweet opportunities of growth, so I would be pre-pared for the life You have planned for me. Keep me in the hollow of Your hand and bless the children You have sent me. Give me wisdom to rear them to become godly citizens of both this world and the next. Thank you for providing this house for me and my little ones. My search-ing is over. There is within the shadow of your loving arms a home for Mandy."

─────────────────────────────

We welcome comments from our readers.
Feel free to write to us at the following address:

Editorial Department
Huntington House Publishers
P.O. Box 53788
Lafayette, LA 70505

or visit our website at:

www.alphapublishingonline.com

─────────────────────────────